"I think you and I have some unfinished business, Mr. Kealoha," she said firmly, attempting to temper the ridiculous pull he had on her.

She was proud of the way her voice came off—strong and confident, not in the least bit revealing the crazy nervousness that quivered within her belly. It was a nervousness she had never, ever felt when dealing with any other legal situation.

"Indeed we do, Ms. Sinclair," he rumbled in his hot-sex-on-a-platter voice. "Please…come in."

She felt something slide over her as he spoke. Oh, yes, she was in trouble.

"Looks like you're going to be busy for a while, Nick. I'll catch up with you later," Lani said.

Sinclair barely registered the woman's presence. Her soft laugh went unheard as Sinclair was engrossed with Nick.

"I'll work on the new figures and we can go over them, later, Lani," Nick murmured, while his hot blue-eyed gaze remained fixed on Sinclair.

Neither one of them noticed when Lani left the room.

Sinclair licked the fuller rim of her bottom lip, her gaze still fixed on Nick.

His eyes were sharply focused on Sinclair. The intensity made her feel off-kilter. Uneasy.

Suddenly, intuitively, she knew what a gazelle felt like when caught in the stare of a hungry, beautiful lion. Dinnertime. And Nick looked like the type that would eat. Her. Whole.

Books by Kimberly Kaye Terry

Harlequin Kimani Romance

Hot to Touch
To Tempt a Wilde
To Love a Wilde
To Desire a Wilde
To Have a Wilde

KIMBERLY KAYE TERRY'S

love for reading romances began at an early age. Long into the night she would stay up with her night-light on until she reached "the end," praying she wouldn't be caught reading what her mother called "those" types of books. Often she would acquire her stash from beneath her mother's bed. Ahem. To date she's an award-winning author of seventeen novels in romance, paranormal romance and erotic romance, and has garnered acclaim for her work. She happily calls writing her full-time job…after chauffeuring around her teenage fashionista daughter, that is.

Kimberly has a bachelor's degree in social work and a master's degree in human relations and has held licenses in social work and mental health therapy in the United States and abroad. She and her daughter volunteer weekly at various social service agencies and she is a long-standing member of Zeta Phi Beta Sorority, Inc., a community-conscious organization. Kimberly is a naturalist and practices aromatherapy. She believes in embracing the powerful woman within each of us and meditates on a regular basis. Kimberly would love to hear from you. Visit her at www.kimberlykayeterry.com.

To Tame a
WILDE

Kimberly Kaye Terry

HARLEQUIN® KIMANI™ ROMANCE

To my beautiful daughter, Hannah, who always inspires
me to be the best that I can be; I love you, Poohma...
now go make up your bed! ;)

Recycling programs
for this product may
not exist in your area.

ISBN-13: 978-0-373-86316-7

TO TAME A WILDE

Copyright © 2013 by Kimberly Kaye Terry

For questions and comments about the quality of this book please contact us
at CustomerService@Harlequin.com.

HARLEQUIN®
™ www.Harlequin.com

Printed in U.S.A.

Dear Reader,

Once again, I would like to thank you for your enthusiasm and love for my Wilde boys and introduce to you the latest Wilde, Nikolaus "Pika" Kealoha, identical twin brother of the very sexy Keanu "Key" Kealoha.

Nick is just as sexy as his twin...and maybe just a little bit more. At least that's what his heroine, the beautiful and savvy corporate attorney Sinclair Adams seems to think. One hot, calculated glance at her from beneath his hooded blue eyes sends her heart beating out control, and her body damp with sexual heat. Heart-pounding tension explodes with their every encounter, starting with the first meeting between Nick and Sinclair, until neither one can take the heat, the pressure...the sexual fire anymore. And when they finally come together, neither will walk away unsinged from the flames.

Kick off your shoes, grab a glass of wine, come on in and enjoy the ride... It's time to saddle up to a Wilde! And as always, be good my wonderful readers. If not...be delicious in your naughty. ;)

~KKT

Chapter 1

Sinclair Adams was tired. No, scratch that. She was damn tired.

"And why am I so blasted tired?" she grumbled.

She briefly closed her eyes and inhaled a fortifying breath before allowing it to softly blow out of her full lips.

She had been expecting a car and driver, supplied by the Kealohas, to meet her at the airport. At least, that is what she had been told would happen.

And yes, a car had been sent—if you could call it a car. The one that had arrived for her shuddered and rattled so badly, she hadn't been the least bit surprised when it just…stopped.

A heartfelt groan slipped from behind her closed lips.

She closed her eyes again, knowing even as the driver,

an older man named Kanoa whose hands had shaken just as badly as the car, turned to her with a resigned look on his aged, weathered face.

"Guess I'd better go check under the hood." His voice registered hopelessness.

He hopped out of the car, spry for his obviously advanced age, and popped the hood. After a lot of noise, tinkering and mild curses, most of which Sinclair didn't understand, he walked to her side of the car and looked at her through the open rear window.

"Miss, I'm sorry, but old Mou Mou here…" Kanoa began, scratching his nearly bald head. "Well, she ain't gonna make it to the hotel. I gotta call a tow."

The look he cast toward the car was so sympathetic as he lovingly patted the rusted roof of…*Mou Mou,* that had Sinclair been in a better frame of mind, she would have felt sorry for the old man. *And* his obviously beloved car.

As it was, she barely checked her irritation. After all, it wasn't the old man's fault. She laid the blame squarely on one person: Nick Kealoha.

She groaned, but her choices were limited. She could either wait for another ride to take her to the hotel— which God only knew how long *that* would take—or climb out of the jalopy and wait alongside the road with Kanoa as the car was towed. She chose the latter, believing it the lesser of two evils and the quickest means to get to the hotel.

By the time she made it to the hotel where Althea Wilde had reserved a room for her, she was tired. And grumpy as all get-out, as her daddy used to say.

"Don't forget that part. I'm tired and I'm mad, and…" She paused in her verbal rant and lifted an arm, daintily taking a sniff as the elevator swiftly ascended. "Lord, I'm sweaty!"

After the elevator made it to her floor, she briskly exited, her high heels sinking into the lush carpeting as she strode down the hall. She slowed her gait, glancing at the slim credit-card-like key in her hand and up at the doors she passed, wanting to locate her room as quickly as possible.

"But at least I'm here," she murmured. Just as she located her suite, she heard a small ding. She glanced down at the Cartier watch, the last gift she'd received from her beloved father before his passing, and muttered a mild curse.

"Could this day get any worse?" she mumbled at the alarm notification. She was supposed to be at the A'kela Ranch in less than an hour.

Thank God she'd allowed Althea to make the reservation. Althea was married to Nathan Wilde—the oldest of her "Wilde Boys," as she collectively called the three men she considered brothers—and the woman was organized to a tee.

"No telling *what* the Kealohas would have had in store for me otherwise," Sinclair huffed as she dragged her suitcase inside the suite.

"Whose fault *is* all of this?" she continued her ranting monologue. To no one in particular.

"Him."

It was all…*his*…fault.

With a disgusted harrumph, her lip curled. She wasn't about to extend *him* the courtesy of saying his name out loud.

Name, image and everything about him had taken up too much of her energy, occupied way too much of her brain time than it should have, she thought, as she hauled her oversize bag inside the room and allowed the door to close softly behind her.

And there was no way she was taking the blame, even if only to herself, for the current state she found herself in.

"The ride-or-die girl herself, Sinclair," she said, releasing another disgusted puff of air from teeth clenched tight. "But…I have to take care of my Wilde Boys," Sinclair said, sighing heavily. "They're family."

She absently glanced around the room, taking it in quickly before dumping bags and her purse on the large king-size bed.

She slumped down on the bed, closing her eyes and arching her sore back.

But it wasn't the Wildes with whom she had issue.

One name, one face, came to mind and claimed *that* number-one spot: Nickolas Kealoha… Nick, as he went by.

Nick, along with his twin brother, Keanu, and father, Alek, owned and operated the A'kela Ranch in Hawaii.

Nickolas Kealoha…Wilde.

And there was the rub—along with the reasons she was far away from home and the Wyoming Wilde Ranch, and now in Hawaii.

Sinclair clenched her eyes tightly closed. And as

usual, what had become irritatingly familiar, the image of Nick Kealoha came to mind. She bit the corner of her lip. She knew what he looked like, every feature down to the lopsided grin he tended to have on his sensual mouth. The way one dimple would appear near his lower lip whenever he would smile, even the slightest bit. In that way he had—

Sinclair quickly opened her eyes, batting them several times as though *that* would scrub the image of Mr. Tall, Golden and Fine from her mind.

"Lord…help me," she muttered and reached down to slip the ridiculously high heels from her feet to massage her arches.

Okay. She was definitely tired. She'd become accustomed to blocking his image from her mind the minute it bombarded its way inside, as though he had every right to take up residence.

Increasingly, his image was the first that came to her mind in the morning as soon as she woke. And it was the last one she visualized at night, right before bed.

Right before dreaming.

"Arggg!" The groan rolled out from between her tightened lips.

She refused to admit how it was affecting her, how his image had been flirting inside her mind for the past several months, relentlessly. Without ceasing.

It had started even before she'd seen his family's show.

As soon as the Wildes had come to her for help with the situation, Sinclair had gone online to check out the

Kealohas in an effort to get an idea of what she would be dealing with. It hadn't been a hard task. As soon as she'd put their name into the search engine on her laptop, pages had filled the screen and she'd clicked through the various links and images. They were, in fact, quite... Google-able. Curious, she'd then decided to check out the show.

"Know thine enemy" had been a saying she had long learned to adhere to, even before completing her law degree. She'd settled down on her sofa and scrolled the various sites before finding the reality show.

That one show had done it....

Oh, Lord. She swallowed deep, the memories making her face burn. Her self-massage came to an abrupt halt, her fingers pausing midrub.

She'd promised herself not to watch another episode. There was absolutely no reason for her to continue, after all. She had watched simply to see the men of the A'kela Ranch—to watch and observe for anything she could use against the Kealohas. Strictly research fodder for her Wilde Boys, no more, no less.

For reasons she refused to analyze, although she'd promised herself *not* to watch another episode, she'd been spellbound. Like a deer caught in headlights, she'd sat on her loveseat watching episode after episode....

And what had started out as a mission simply to "know her enemy," had turned into a marathon TV session that had her viewing both seasons one and two of the popular cable network show. Episodes where Nick seemed to be most present, she'd watched twice. Sometimes three times.

The man was drop-dead fine as hell, no two ways about it.

After that, his image had been scored into her brain, from his golden-boy good looks to the bright blue eyes that seemed to show mischief even if the camera wasn't aimed in his direction. Even if he wasn't the one the scene was focused on, he seemed to attract all the attention to his broad shoulders, narrow waist and muscled thighs that even behind the signature rugged jeans he wore couldn't disguise the masculine appeal.

All of him had captured Sinclair's attention. And although she should have been irritated at the way he seemed to know it, the way he carried himself as though he was the only man on the planet, alpha to the nth degree…she'd found herself getting wet. Just from looking at him.

Sinclair had noticed that although the show featured the Kealoha ranch, the actual *Kealohas,* both brothers as well as father, were rarely on camera. However, when Nick glanced into the camera and spoke, it was as though he was speaking directly to her.

She felt a tangible…warmth invade her body. Sexual. Predatory heat…

Ingrained into her mind was the way his low-hooded, intense blue eyes would glance into the camera…his sculpted cheeks… And the hint of a dimple that would appear near his lower lip when he gave that ghost of a smile that Sinclair now associated with pure, raw, masculine…sex.

She sucked in a deep breath of air.

It all screamed that he was a man who knew his way around a woman's body.

Her face flushed. Her panties grew wet.

Hot mess? Nah…she was *way* past that.

"Uhhhh!" The growl of frustration slipped from her lips and Sinclair quickly snapped her eyes open and batted them profusely.

She needed help.

Nick Kealoha was a player. Straight. Up. Player.

No two ways around it. It was all in his image. The way he carried himself. She'd read his bio…and she was not going to be played. Never had, never would.

Sinclair straightened her spine and tossed her hair back over her shoulder. She ignored the way her thick, wavy curls refused to behave, and how the once-straight strands were a memory of the past.

She ran a hand over her hair and circled the bunch in one hand. After opening a pocket of her messenger bag she'd tossed on the bed, she withdrew a covered band and deftly secured the thick, dense mass of curls.

No. *She* did not see him as one part of the "dynamic duo" that he and his twin had so cheesily been dubbed by the media.

She only saw the irritating man she had come to truly…have issue with.

Their communication had begun when Sinclair had taken over all dealings with the Kealohas immediately after Nick's initial terse letter to the family, demanding retribution.

Although the Wildes, as well as Sinclair, had been surprised to find out that their adoptive father, Clint Jedediah Wilde, had fathered a set of twins more than thirty years ago, they had been happy, ready to meet their "brothers" and to hear their story.

Unfortunately, it wasn't long after that that they realized the Kealohas, in particular Nick Kealoha, was not exactly in the "family reunion" sort of mood. His demand was concise, to the point. He and his brother were demanding they get what was theirs legally: interest in the Wyoming Wilde Ranch.

"Not even gonna happen," had been the collective response from her Wilde Boys, big arms crossed over their large chests, faces set.

Although she didn't feel like smiling, the image of the big men, hard looks across their handsome faces, brought a smile to her face.

Although the Wildes were adoptive brothers, sharing no blood link, the men were just about as close as three brothers could be. And when they felt threatened it was quite an impressive sight to see them rally together.

Ready to kick ass first and take names later, if necessary, as Holt Wilde had once so eloquently put it.

Not that it would come to that, Sinclair had assured them, confident in her abilities as a mediator and the speed with which she'd contacted the Kealohas. In particular, Nick Kealoha.

Soon, her confidence had taken a radical turn.

With their first correspondence via email she'd known she was in trouble. She'd immediately sought out verbal communication after his rude response to what she'd viewed as a perfectly reasonable request for a meeting.

He'd ignored her, as well as her request for a meeting, to the point she'd felt every one of her back teeth would grind down to dust in her frustration from dealing with the irritating man.

Finally she'd gotten him on the phone and sparks had flown swiftly, strongly. After hanging up, Sinclair had felt as though she'd been skinned alive.

She'd felt…unnerved by the man. His voice had been the first thing to cause the dichotomy of feelings.

Low, sexy…rough.

She'd felt her heart slam against her rib cage, but had forced the crazy reaction to the side.

This was war. And from the get-go, he'd identified himself as the enemy.

Shelving the odd feelings, she'd at first wanted to walk away, but had known she couldn't, that she wouldn't.

She was not only the Wildes' lawyer, she was…family. There was nothing she would *not* do for her Wilde Boys. With resignation she'd gone to work, seeking to find out what she could about the Kealohas.

It hadn't been hard. As soon as she'd discovered they'd had their own reality show, the information had been relatively easy to acquire.

Not that she'd had to go that far for info. As soon as she'd plugged their name into her search engine, there had been pages and pages of information. And images…

For as much information as she'd uncovered about the men and their ranch, there had been just as many images, if not more. Identical twins who not only ran the most successful family-owned-and-operated ranch in Hawaii, but were also drop-dead fine? Yeah…there'd not been a shortage of images.

From the moment she'd laid eyes on him, she'd known Nick Kealoha was going to be impossible to deal with.

"And I was right," she murmured. "And now…time to face the devil," she whispered as she got up off the bed. And heard the excitement…fear in her voice.

That was the sum total of what she *would* allow herself to think about: the fact that he was nothing but an irritant. A sexy-as-hell irritant, but nonetheless an irritant. One she would deal with swiftly and be done with.

A mocking little laugh echoed in her ear. She swatted it away with her hand as though that would make *it,* and the reason for *it,* disappear. Nothing more than a nuisance.

Sinclair swiftly opened her suitcase and withdrew clothes to change into. Time was of the essence. She'd do a quick refresh and be out.

She ruthlessly tamped down the annoying fissure of delight she felt curling through her spine.

This was just a meeting. A meeting where she would do the best she could to make sure her Wilde Boys were not milked and taken for what was theirs, if not by true birthright, then by sweat, blood and tears.

Sinclair ignored the excited sliver of…*something*… that rushed over her at the thought. *Something* she refused to name. Yet, try as she might, that also refused to go away.

She hadn't met the man…. The thought occurred to her that by coming to the Kealoha ranch in Hawaii, she just might have bitten off more than she was willing to chew.

Even that thought excited her.

No one was taking anything from her boys, not if Sinclair had anything to say about it. And if that meant taking on the devil himself, she was just the woman for the job.

Chapter 2

Nick Kealoha frowned, his eyes scanning the computer screen, rereading the latest correspondence via email from the Wildes' attorney.

For the third time.

A sneer kicked the corner of his mouth upward into parody of a smile. The fools hadn't wanted to deal with him, so they'd sicced their lawyer on him.

"Damn woman," he grumbled as he strummed the fingers of one large, long-fingered hand absently against his desk. The other hand was poised over the keyboard as he thought about what he *should* have said instead of what he had said in response to the email.

As he reread the lawyer's message, despite his self-avowals to the contrary, the woman was getting to him.

That self-admission alone ticked him off.

His eyes studied the email from Sinclair Adams, the attorney for the Wilde Ranch of Wyoming.

Greetings Mr. Kealoha,

After consulting with the Wildes, I am informing you of the family's wish for a more personal approach in dealing with our...situation. Unfortunately, over the course of the past week you have ignored my certified mail as well as ignored my phone calls, and I feel as though the situation is degenerating versus improving. To prevent a complete breakdown in communication, and to continue with the path we've been on—resolution—we, the Wildes and I, feel it is best for a one-on-one approach. To this end, please expect a visit from me to the A'kela Ranch. It is our sincere hope that you and your family will be able to meet with me so that we may resolve this matter to the satisfaction of all parties. I will arrive Tuesday of next week in the hope that you and your family will work with me to resolve this matter.

Best,

Sinclair Adams, PLLC

He'd received the correspondence, spoken to his brother about it and promptly dismissed the woman from his mind.

Or tried to.

"Lot of damn good *that* did," he muttered.

He'd known she was on her way to the island. Known about it and hadn't told his family about it until it was too late for either his brother or father to call the Wildes or their lawyer to settle the matter.

He'd even told her he would send a driver for her.

He wanted her here, on his territory.

A feral grin split his mouth into a smile.

From the beginning of his…interaction with Ms. Sinclair Adams, Nick had found himself in a state of semi-arousal.

Didn't much matter when it happened. Whenever he either thought of the irritating woman or had *any* type of contact—written, emailed or verbal—his body reacted.

Hell, he could just listen to his voice mail and his cock was hard as granite.

The one time they'd had the Skype conversation…

Damn.

Even as he thought about it now, his cock hardened and his balls tightened in memory.

He'd seen pictures of her plenty. He'd known what she looked like, and had been intrigued. She had a different kind of beauty. Not traditional, but no less hot to him.

Then they'd spoken on the phone. They'd had conversations that had left him wanting…more. But the video interaction had taken it to another level.

Their conversation had been heated and he'd alternated between wanting *her* and wanting to strangle her pretty little neck. As soon as he'd gone to bed that night, he'd relived their exchange and the whole "wanting her" part had taken over.

And he'd promptly had one of the hottest dreams he'd

had as an adult male. He had woken up with his shaft, again, in his hand, his seed spilled over his stomach.

With a mild curse he'd reached over, pulled open the side table drawer and withdrawn a napkin, which he now kept at the ready for that very reason.

He'd had more wet dreams over the past few months because of her than he'd had, collectively, as a randy teenage boy.

It had gotten to the point he was beginning to think she'd cast some kind of spell on him. He'd never been so worked up over a woman he'd never met in person, much less one who was in the enemy camp, so to speak.

As soon as she'd begun to communicate with him, he'd researched who she was.

His initial thought had simply been to go by the creed of "know thine enemy." But it had turned into something…more.

Although calling the Wildes his enemy was a bit of a stretch. His anger had actually cooled toward the deception his mother had kept hidden for all those years: that he and his brother were the product of an illicit affair.

He cursed, low, his voice barely audible.

And no matter what his feelings toward Jed Wilde, whether he'd known about his and Key's existence or not, it wasn't his true father's—Alek Kealoha's—fault.

In fact, he'd been ready to call it off, and just let it all go. It wasn't as though he really wanted anything Jed Wilde had, or anything he'd left to his adoptive sons. Nick and his family had a ranch that was just as impressive and in no way needed anything the Wildes had. They were doing damn fine on their own.

He'd even told both his father and brother the same thing, much to the relief of both. They, too, didn't want anything the Wildes had, nor were they interested in dredging up old family dirt. They'd come to a resolution about it all, and now that both Clint Jedediah Wilde and their mother, A'kela Kealoha, had passed away, there was no need to protect anyone.

Even though there was still a small part of Nick that wanted to know what kind of man Jed had been, in the end, neither he nor Key wanted to hurt the man they'd called Father for their entire lives.

Yet, after the first encounter with Sinclair Adams, what he had found out about her through his amateur sleuthing had left him wanting to know more. So much so that he'd continued his threats.

Just because of her.

He wouldn't call himself a research nut by any means, but he damn well knew how to find out about a person if need be. He had taken to the internet in the hope that he'd learn more about her, assuming she was some high-powered attorney.

What he'd learned had left him even more intrigued.

The Wildes were easy to research. He'd simply entered the name of the ranch and, presto, a virtual flood of information was at his fingertips. It had taken a while, but he'd eventually uncovered information about Sinclair.

Pictures of her on the Wilde Ranch had shown a

young woman he didn't believe could possibly be the sophisticated woman portrayed in both the smooth-toned voice mails she'd left on his phone and the succinct emails she'd sent.

Further stealth-mode investigation had showed that it was indeed the same woman. Not only was she on the Wildes' website, there had been a hyperlink that directed him to her own website. Her bio had been impressive.

She appeared young, too young for the accomplishments listed in her biography. He'd frowned. Although young, she'd built quite a name for herself in her area of expertise in law.

Now working primarily as the lawyer for the Wildes, from what Nick had been able to learn from his internet search, she'd also had dealings in corporate law. She had interned with a prestigious law firm in Cheyenne, Wyoming, before returning home. She'd listed the Wyoming Wilde Ranch as home and he'd frowned, wondering if she had grown up on the ranch.

Just as on the A'Kela Ranch, Nick knew that many of the larger, successful ranches had generations of family members that worked and lived on the ranch. He'd guessed she was a family member.

He'd reached out and called her. In a voice low and sexy, feminine yet husky, she'd had him hard as hell, sitting up in his seat and listening intently to the low-toned voice smoothly inform him of her clients' wish to settle this unfortunate incident with as little "fanfare" as possible.

It had taken a minute for the insult to register.

And now, after four months of cyber interacting, she was on her way to the ranch. All that cyber *interacting* had him on edge.

He felt his cock stir at the thought. Unconsciously he adjusted himself within his jeans. If she made him feel in person even the *slightest* bit as she had during their previous interactions—verbal heated conversations, sharply worded yet oddly arousing emails and voice mails… He shook his head.

Hell, yeah. Things were about to get really interesting around the Kealoha ranch.

As he told his brother about his dealings with Sinclair Adams, Key remained silent throughout the conversation, down to Nick's informing his twin of the woman's upcoming arrival.

After he finished speaking, he waited.

It hadn't taken long.

"What?" Nick asked, mildly irritated and somewhat unnerved by his twin's silence and sharp regard—two things he didn't necessarily like linked when it came to his brother and his uncanny ability to know what was on Nick's mind.

Key simply raised a thick brow and shrugged, coffee mug in hand, his gaze steady and intense.

"What *what?* I didn't say anything," Key replied. He brought the rim of his coffee mug to his mouth and took a casual sip, his eyes still focused on Nick.

Nick's brows bunched.

"Nothing to say, bro?"

"What do you want me to say?" Key threw back the question, shrugging. "I have better things to do. Besides, you know my stance on that situation."

Nick pushed away from the counter where he'd been lounging, feigning a nonchalance he was far from feeling, and just as casually as his brother, refilled his coffee mug.

"Better things to do? Like you and Sonia producing the next generation of Kealohas?"

Two could play the game. Just as Key had an eerie ability to know what was going on with him, Nick could do the same with his twin.

One of the many perks of being an identical twin and for that same twin to be his best friend.

If he wasn't in such a *mood,* he'd laugh at the expression on Key's face.

"How did you…" Key began, only to stop. He shook his head and barked out a laugh instead. "Never mind."

Nick laughed along with his brother, breaking the tension. He then went on to tell him the details of Sinclair's impending arrival.

After listening to Key cuss a blue streak, telling Nick what he thought of his lack of brains, to put it mildly, for not letting the family know "what the hell was going on," the two men sat at the kitchen table.

Although he really wasn't up for a "*Dr Phil*" moment, Nick had haltingly opened up, slightly, to his brother. He was glad when his brother finally reacted.

He'd spared Key the more embarrassing details. Hell,

there was no sense in telling his brother what was going on with him. He wasn't sure what was going on in his own psyche, anyway. And to go into confusing feelings for a woman he hardly knew…? No. That wasn't going to happen.

He laughed even thinking about it. He could only imagine how Key would look at him. Nick had never really been the type of guy to share his thoughts that easily. Even with his brother, the closest person in the world to him, Nick was still, at times, the clam.

But there had been times in his life, like now, where he'd felt a real need to break the mold. So he opened up a little, at least enough to tell Key that he wasn't sure how to handle the situation with Sinclair. He'd known he'd have to come clean, if nothing else, to get a feel for his brother's take on the situation.

As he spoke, Key listened, not saying a word. When Nick finished his succinct tale, Key stood from the table and slapped his brother on the back…hard.

"I'm sure you can handle it, bro. In fact, I know you will," he stated, his voice emphatic, a tinge of humor laced in.

Nick sat back, puzzled.

His brother continued. "I'm so confident in your abilities that on behalf of the family I'm *giving* this to you." The evil gleam in his brother's eyes, blue eyes that matched his own, should have given Nick fair warning. "Consider this…'situation' solely your deal. Dad and I are out of it. I'm sure you'll figure it all out."

Again, his brother smacked him on the back.

"What the fu—" Nick bit off the curse, jumping up after his brother's hearty smack on the back, toppling his chair as he rose. Swiftly he righted the chair and turned to face his brother.

"What the hell, man…that's *it?*" he asked, staring at his twin as he calmly walked to the sink, coffee mug in hand.

"Yep. That's it, Pika," Key replied, snorting.

Whenever his brother used his nickname, it always set Nick's teeth on edge. Not because he didn't like his nickname… He'd been called Pika, which meant "strong" in the Polynesian language, since he was a boy.

Nicknames were nothing new. Key's legal name was Keanu, but he'd been called Key for most of his life. It irritated Nick because he knew there were times when Key used the nickname simply to screw with him. Something both men considered their God-given right to do: give his twin a hard time.

Nick had always thought of it as good old-fashioned fun. Until he was on the receiving end.

Just as Key placed the coffee mug in the sink to rinse—*no one* wanted to deal with their housekeeper, Mahi, the longest resident of the ranch outside of the family, and his rants if the kitchen was left a mess— Sonia, his wife, entered.

She quickly spied her husband. A wide grin split her pretty face as she made a beeline for her new husband and wrapped her arms around his waist.

"Hmm, last night was amazing, baby," Sonia purred,

her voice low, throaty and intimate, once Key released the death grip he had on his wife's lips.

"It's been way too long, baby," she murmured as Key reached down and captured her lips again. Finally he released her, enough to glance down at her, keeping her within the circle of his arms.

"Yeah, it felt like forever," Key agreed, his voice barely recognizable it was so low.

Key had been away on an overnight trip, so really it hadn't been that long, Nick thought, shaking his head.

"Little Alek isn't going to magically appear, you know. It's going to take dedication and hard…" He paused and unashamedly pressed his wife close to his body, allowing her to feel which part of hard he was referring to. "Work," Key murmured, stopping to give Sonia kisses down the line of her throat. "And work…" He paused again to capture an earlobe.

Nick wanted to throw something at the pair…maybe cold water. They were like two dogs in heat.

"And work," his brother *finally* finished. His voice was so low Nick suddenly felt uncomfortable.

He felt like a damn voyeur and desperately wanted to get the hell away from the pair. Yet… Against his will, he was fascinated with their play. He watched as his brother bent to kiss away the frown that appeared on his wife's brow before slanting his mouth over her lips.

"Oh, yeah?" she asked huskily when he released her mouth. Although she was obviously trying hard to keep the smile from her mouth, the dimple in her cheek flashed against her will.

"And who says *she* is going to be a *he?*" she asked with a shrug. "We could have a little A'kela in the cards for us," she said. But the look in her eyes told the real story. Just like his brother, Nick knew his sister-in-law didn't care either way, boy or girl.

Nick *had* to glance away; the intense look of love in his brother's eyes was too much for him to see and not react. And right now he wanted to be pissed at his twin. Not want to hug him.

It was no secret that the couple was trying to have a baby. Neither was it a secret that if the baby was a girl, it would be named after their mother, and if it was a boy, it would be named after their father.

He turned back to the couple and caught the soft look in Key's eyes and the small smile that graced the corners of his mouth as he steadily regarded his wife of six months.

Had he not loved his brother so much, and truly loved Sonia like a sister, he would feel real envy for the couple. Their love was so tangible; it wasn't unheard of for one or usually both of them to be totally oblivious of anyone else in the room when they were around each other.

Deep and real.

He turned to leave and would have made it away had he not bumped into the chair he'd just righted, sending it crashing to the floor. He bit off a curse and picked it up.

"Hey, Nick, I didn't see you there!" Sonia said, a deep stain of color washing over her sienna-colored skin as she realized he'd caught them in an intimate moment.

He grinned widely.

"Not like I haven't seen you two like this before… disgustingly lost in the moment," he grumbled playfully, not sparing her. She was family. The Family That Teased Together Stayed Together was his motto.

"In fact, I don't think I'll be able to look at the hot tub *or* the pool again in the same way after last week," he said. He hadn't really seen anything. But he'd hazarded a guess that, knowing his brother, something illicit had taken place in the hot tub. Without a doubt. He'd bet his last dollar on the fact they'd gotten busy there.

He brought his attention back to the pair.

His sister-in-law's eyes opened wide and her head jerked, looking up at Key. Key leaned down, allowing his mouth to hover near her ear.

She blushed even harder at whatever his brother whispered in her ear, halfheartedly slapping away the hand that rested on her butt.

"Key!" she admonished, voice low, yet Nick clearly heard the sensuality in it. "Stop it, we can't… I have work to do," she stammered, but when he leaned down to whisper something else in her ear, her eyes widened and she bit the lower rim of her lip.

"Really? We can try that?" She gnawed on her lip, as though considering whatever it was his brother had proposed. "Okay…I'm game if you are. I can do edits later today," she said, the blush growing. "Or tomorrow," she finished and, giggling, allowed his brother to lead her away.

Leaving Nick to stare after them, shaking his head. Freaks.

The grin returned to his face, but soon thoughts of Sinclair filtered back into his brain and how he'd *deal* with her.

And from the look of things, he'd not be getting any help from his family in "handling" the situation.

Which was perfectly okay with him, considering how…deviant he knew he could sometimes be.

He chuckled at the thought.

Good. He was flying solo. That had always worked best for him. It was best for others, even family, who probably didn't know *just* how wicked he could be.

It was time to work on his plan.

Chapter 3

Nick pinched the high bridge of his nose and pulled his glasses away from his face, frowning deeply.

"What's the problem, old man? Sight not as good as it used to be?"

Startled, believing himself alone, his thoughts still on Sinclair, Nick glanced up and away from the computer screen to see his foreman standing in his office doorway, arms folded over her breasts, eyebrow raised.

"Hmm… Last time I checked, you weren't that far behind me in age, Alli-oop," he replied sardonically, a small grin threatening to break free. "What's up? Come on in," he said, waving Ailani Mowry inside his office.

"Don't want to interrupt," she drawled, yet pushed away from the doorway and ambled inside his office nonetheless.

"Hell, it's not like I'm getting any work done, anyway," he growled. Although he wasn't about to disclose the true reason for his malcontent, he couldn't keep the irritation away from his voice.

He glanced at the monitor and realized Sinclair's picture filled the *entire* screen. He could only imagine Ailani's reaction if she saw that image as his screen saver. Like he needed that.

Swiftly, casually, he minimized the screen and maximized the previous screen he'd been viewing: a PDF showing the projected budget revenues for the upcoming quarter.

No sooner had the spreadsheet appeared on the screen than Ailani was standing beside the desk, peering over his shoulder.

"Looks like we're going to be up in revenue significantly for the upcoming quarter," she commented and, without asking, grabbed for the small chair near the desk. She dragged it over closer to his chair, her eyes never leaving contact with the monitor.

He glanced over at her as she peered at the screen, completely ignoring him and the chair. Ailani and he shared history. No two ways about it, she was a beautiful woman, even as she "hid" her beauty.

More often than not she was seen wearing her long thick hair in a tight French braid tucked beneath the battered pink cowboy hat she'd worn since the beginning of time.

Many had thought the two of them would end up together. But despite growing up together from the time they were children, and the short stint where they'd shared a romance, the two had maintained a platonic relationship.

He continued to watch her as her eyes darted over the graph. When she turned to face him, although her eyes were hidden behind the tinted glasses she typically wore to shield her sensitive eyes, he caught the scrutiny.

"So, tell me. What were you really looking at with such intensity when I walked in, Pika?" she asked, a smirk creasing the corner of her small mouth. "And don't tell me it was this projection. It's not even the one from this quarter," she noted, crossing her arms over her ample breasts and waiting.

His eyes flew to the screen. Sure enough, instead of the PDF showing the budget for the upcoming quarter, it was the one from the last quarter.

Damn. His head was most definitely not in the game.

Just as he had with his brother, he feigned a nonchalance he was far from feeling and tried to play it off.

"Comparing last month's feed budget projection with the actual cost, cross-comparing it with the upcoming fiscal year's budget to determine if we need to reevaluate the project. And if so, do we need to make cuts in other areas to make up the difference."

His response was quick and *sounded* knowledgeable.

He hoped she actually *bought* his bullshit.

There was silence for longer than Nick liked, yet he kept his eyes glued to the screen.

Ailani leaned forward and brought her body closer to his. A hint of patchouli and hibiscus wafted across his nose; a scent she'd been wearing for as long as he could remember.

She jabbed a short but manicured nail at the screen, pointing to one of the columns.

"Who came up with this projection? No way is this budget anywhere near what we're looking at for the upcoming quarter, nor does it make any sense for the new fiscal year!" she huffed, her eyes scanning the document on the screen. "Between the hike in prices in grain and feed, as well as the new shipment of steers we purchased last year, we're looking at a number substantially higher than this," she proclaimed.

Nick breathed a sigh of relief.

An irritated Ailani was much more preferable to a discerning one.

Of everyone he was acquainted with, besides his twin, Ailani was one of the most astute individuals he knew. If she caught even a *sniff,* a *whiff,* that something wasn't quite right, she'd hunt it down. The woman could teach his father's best hounds the true art of the hunt.

Lucky for him, her hound-dog nose was holstered for the present.

She wasn't paying much attention to him; her attention was purely on the ranch's budget.

Despite himself, he bit back a grin. Good thing he now thought of Ailani like a sister, or her lack of attention would have been insulting.

She leaned even closer, the right side of her breast brushing against his shoulder.

"What are you thinking with these projections?

Geesh, what would you do without me, Pika? Knuckle-head…" she grumbled, pushing even closer, the side of her breast nearly colliding with his nose.

"I know you want me and all, but really, Ailani, could you get your damn boob outta my face?" he complained roughly. He barked out a laugh when she distractedly batted a hand at him, ignoring him as she continued to peruse the document.

"If I didn't know any better, I would think I didn't do anything for you, Ailani…but we both know that isn't true. What with you practically nursing me and all," he continued, knowing she wasn't paying much attention to what he said.

"Pika," she mumbled, her voice completely distracted. *"Whatever,"* she finished, dragging out the word, the frown on her face growing.

Without looking behind her, she blindly reached for the chair she'd dragged to his desk earlier. Moving it closer, she plopped down in the seat.

As she examined the document, Nick continued to make completely inappropriate, off-color comments to Ailani, chuckling when she continued to ignore his bait-ing.

If she even heard it. Which he doubted she did.

When it came to her job as ranch foreman, all else became background noise to her. Which made it even more fun for Nick to tease her.

Just as he grinned and opened his mouth to make yet *another* inappropriate comment about her boob pressing into his face, a cough at the door caught his attention.

"One of your men told me you were alone. But if I'm interrupting, I can…you know, come back later."

His eyes flew to the door and the grin slowly slipped from his face.

He jumped from his chair like a soldier would when his commanding officer entered. So fast that his chair shot out from under him and probably would have toppled over had Ailani not caught it.

Not that he was giving his foreman any attention.

That honor went solely to the woman who had claimed more of his attention than she had any right to.

The woman who had him waking up in the morning, rock-hard shaft in his hand, finishing off the job she'd started. If only in his dreams.

Her voice alone brought his cock to full-on "salute" status. Just like the good soldier that it was.

Husky and low…it poured over him like scalding rain. Even as it held a chastising note, it was turning him on in ways he'd never experienced from simply listening to a woman's voice.

Hell, maybe that whole chastising tone she had going on added to the overall effect.

Whatever it was, it—*she*—had him hooked.

Her voice was velvety smooth and sexy, the type that reminded him of rainy days and sleeping in with a lover. But then his glance ran over her, head to toe. As hot as her voice was, it was nothing compared to her body.

Damn.

Live and in living color. On his turf… With no more provocation than that, his cock stirred.

Although he'd only seen pictures of her from the internet, those pictures were scorched permanently into his mind.

One of those images came to mind. The one he'd found of her at the Wildes' ranch and had printed out on the spur of the moment. The same one he'd glanced at just last night before he'd succumbed to sleep.

The dream spurred from that image had been one that had haunted him as he'd wakened. His cock hardened even more as his gaze raked over her now.

There was no denying who stood in his doorway, one arched brow raised, small bow-shaped lips pursed, stiletto-heeled foot tapping.

Sinclair Adams.

Chapter 4

Confrontation time.

Sinclair kept her expression tight.

Closed.

Control… She had to keep it around her like a security blanket.

She was afraid if she didn't, she would lose it.

Control was her best friend. Especially now. Thoughts of what her last few hours had been like, from the time she'd arrived in Hawaii and the fiasco surrounding all of *that*…to now, as she observed the scene in front of her. In one all-encompassing swoop, from the large office with its floor-to-ceiling windows that faced a gorgeous picturesque scene straight out of a movie, to the desk in the center of the room…and the commanding man who sat behind it.

There was also a beautiful woman with massive breasts standing close by... Sinclair took it all in. Okay, so maybe she was being catty. The woman's breasts weren't all that *massive*.

No matter, she thought, tightly reining in her envy.

She was squarely in the middle of the enemy's camp. She felt her back stiffen as she lifted her chin, automatically "preparing." For what? She would wait and see.

Her gaze made a swift survey of the office, taking special note of the custom-built book cabinets and the obviously expensive furnishings.

The walls were painted a muted deep red. One wall was nothing but an assortment of mirrors in various sizes and shapes.

Bold decorating choice, just like the red. The color choice and the mirrors were oddly erotic to her.

She shook her head, negating the thought before it had a chance to bloom any further in her mind. She continued her quick assessment.

There was an array of beautiful oversize rugs covering the polished hardwood floor, and a variety of artfully arranged statues that she would love to get a closer look at, had she been here for any other reason than the reason she was.

She brought herself up short.

She hadn't come to the Kealoha ranch to admire the beautiful furnishings, the amazing scenery...or the exotic-looking woman who was now staring at her as though she knew her.

She was here for business. She turned her attention to the man she'd come to do battle with.

And that is exactly what it was in her mind: a battle. Her eyes narrowed as she watched the woman standing so close to him.

And it definitely wasn't any of her business who the woman was. The same woman whose breasts—breasts that Sinclair doubted were her own—had been pressed against the side of Nick Kealoha's face as if she were about to breast-feed the man, when Sinclair had approached the door.

Sinclair knew she was being unfair; she didn't know the woman. For all she knew the massive boobs could actually belong to the woman. She mentally shrugged, pretending not to feel the least bit of *anything* about the woman, her breasts, or where they had been pressed....

Nor the man they had been pressed against. Not really. None of that mattered.

She was just feeling a tad bit...irked. She took in a physical and figurative breath and silently recited one of her favorite quick-but-calming mantras. It took a few seconds longer than normal, but she got it together.

She turned her gaze to Nickolas Kealoha, after nodding to the woman next to him. His gaze was already locked and loaded on hers.

This time, the breath she took was anything but figurative. Nickolas Kealoha was breath-stealingly fine.

Bright blue eyes kept her regard from beneath thick lashes, lashes that from the distance she was from him seemed impossible...ridiculous for a man to possess.

Even though he was sitting behind the desk, the sheer...massiveness of the man was enough to make her breath catch at the back of her throat. She had to remind herself to breathe. In. Out. In...

Big arms, thick with bulging muscle, were pressed against the desk. His chest seemed carved from granite. She bit back the moan when she caught sight of the small tuft of hair that splayed from beneath the fitted black T-shirt he wore under his chambray shirt.

Her gaze cataloged the long, muscular, thick thighs that even the simple work jeans he wore couldn't disguise. At his lean waist he wore a belt and large buckle with some type of crest. From her vantage point she couldn't tell what exactly was depicted on the belt buckle.

Because, yes...she was only interested in his belt buckle and most definitely not the thick...outline...that lay just south of the buckle.

"Like I said... If I'm interrupting *anything*..." she repeated. She cleared her throat and allowed the sentence to dangle.

"Of course not," the woman cut in, before Nick could say a word. "I was just leaving."

Sinclair saw him cut the woman a quick glance, no doubt cataloguing the shit-eating grin on her face, just as Sinclair had seen the sly look on the other woman's face, as well. It hinted at a long association, a certain familiarity.

Sinclair noted the obvious closeness between the two, for future reference.

And completely forced herself to ignore the ugly stab of jealousy she felt. Along with the immediate desire to swipe the grin from the woman's face.

The woman grabbed the pink beat-up Stetson that sat on Nick's oversize desk and jammed it onto her head, grabbing the thick ponytail and negligently tossing the thick rope of hair in front of her shoulder, so that the ends dangled beneath her breasts.

The movement was so quick and casual, Sinclair knew that it was one the woman did a lot, without thought.

"Yes, please come on in. Ms. Adams, I presume?" Nick asked casually, one thick eyebrow raised in question, as though unsure who she was. At the same time his eyes roamed over her as though she was dessert on the dinner menu.

Sinclair clenched her lower jaw so tightly she feared she'd need an emergency visit to the dentist if she wasn't careful.

She inhaled a deep, fortifying breath.

Control, Sinclair… Control, she reminded herself. She was here for her Wilde Boys, and that was it. As soon as this was over she was out.

She simply had to remind herself of that fact.

"Ms. Adams?" he asked again, and Sinclair's eyes met his. He stood and began to walk toward her, his stride long, purposeful.

As though against her will, she backed up a fraction. When her back hit the door she stopped, embarrassed.

Even from across the room, it was as though his piercing blue eyes were drilling a hole into her.

He came closer, his long legs eating up the short distance in mere seconds. He stopped less than a foot away from where she stood in the doorway, his gaze leisurely traveling over her face and down the length of her exposed neck...to the deep V juncture of her silky blouse.

His eyes lingered on the swell of her breasts.

As though he had every right.

Sinclair cleared her throat.

"Please...come in," he murmured, voice low. Sexy.

She felt a shiver run over her body.

His eyes finally moved back up to lock with hers.

Sinclair fought with everything she had to keep her eyes open. It was as though an odd lethargy had invaded her body and the strange pull he had on her increased.

They had spoken on the phone many times, and his voice had captured her attention from the beginning. They'd even had that unforgettable Skype experience, one that still made her blush because of what she'd done that night, alone in bed, thinking of him and his deep, rumbling voice and handsome face. But seeing and hearing *him* live?

Dear God. The fascination she'd had...the pull he'd had on her.... The one that had been increasing over the past six months of their association was set to detonate. She could feel it.

It was a low, rich rumble that resonated through her body, catching her completely off guard.

It surrounded her.

Sinclair's eyes briefly closed, no longer able to fight it...

As though touching her, his voice reached out and...

caressed her. *Did things to her.* She felt a trickle of moisture dampen her panties.

A shiver of awareness slithered down her body and she struck out her tongue to dampen lips that had gone completely dry.

"Sinclair." His deep, rich voice made her heart catch. She forced her eyes open and realized he was close. Too close.

Back up! she silently yelled—begged—him.

She felt claustrophobic.

Her gaze met the level of his throat. His neck, thickly corded with muscle, worked as he seemed to swallow.

Immediately her breasts reacted. Heavy, they felt engorged, her nipples pressing urgently against the thin silk of her brassiere. One she should have thought twice about wearing, as it had about as much protection against the heat of his stare as a thong in a snowstorm.

It was as though she knew this man…really knew him. On a level that made no sense to her.

It makes no damn sense, Sinclair! she silently screamed at herself.

Come on…his throat is sexy, a mocking voice piped in, laughing at her.

As soon as the thought entered her mind, Sinclair rejected it. She dragged her eyes away from his throat. Since when did she find a man's throat sexy?

Frick!

Okay. Control. *Bring back the control, girl,* she admonished herself.

But, God… The combination of his voice and those

hypnotic blue eyes, along with his impossibly handsome face…not to mention his body—big, hovering, masculine body. It all summed up to making her feel like a house cat in heat. Trapped, with no outlet.

She hadn't been in the least bit afraid to bring the battle to *their* camp. She was just that type of woman. Bold. Without conceit she knew she could handle hers when it came to any sort of…battle. So when it had come time to battle the Kealohas, Nick in particular, she'd not thought twice about it. She had, in fact, relished the idea after months of dealing with the stubborn man.

Yet for a moment she wished to God she could reverse time. Rethink her "you don't know with whom you're messing" decision to fly to Hawaii and confront the Kealohas.

But she had no time for a redo.

She had to deal with the situation. And deal she would. She'd never been the type of woman who was afraid of a man, fine or not.

She placed a faux smile on her face and pushed away from the door. Allowing him to usher her inside, she walked in front of him, trying for a nonchalance she was far, *far* from feeling.

She was glad she'd decided against throwing on her flats. The five-inch pumps she was wearing were just what she needed to help give her a bit of an edge.

She knew his eyes were glued on her butt as she walked ahead of him.

She put just a hint of something extra in her walk

and shrugged on her confidence as she would her favorite sweater.

"I think you and I have some unfinished business, Mr. Kealoha," she said, firmly tamping down the ridiculous pull he had on her.

She was proud of the way her voice came off. Strong, confident…and not in the least bit showing the crazy nervousness that quivered within her belly.… A nervousness she'd never, ever felt when dealing with any other legal situation.

"Indeed we do, Ms. Sinclair," he rumbled in his "hot sex on the platter" voice. She felt…*something* slide over her as he spoke.

She turned to face him. Oh, yes… She was in trouble.

"Looks like you're going to be busy for a while, Nick… I'll catch up with you later," the pink-hatted woman said as she made her way to the door.

Sinclair barely registered her presence.

The woman laughed softly as she left, saying something that Sinclair didn't even catch, she was so caught up in…him. It was as though no one else was in the room.

"I'll work on the new figures and we can go over them later, Lani," she heard Nick murmur to the woman, yet his hot blue-eyed gaze remained fixed on her.

Neither one of them noticed when the woman left the room, quietly closing the door behind her.

Sinclair licked her bottom lip, her gaze still fixed on Nick.

His scrutiny was sharp, focused, the intensity making her feel off-kilter. Uneasy.

Suddenly, intuitively, she knew what a gazelle felt like caught in the stare of a lion.... A hungry, beautiful lion.

Dinnertime. And he looked like the type that would... Eat. Her. Whole.

She swallowed.

Chapter 5

The first thought that came to Nick's mind was that her pictures didn't do her justice.

The woman was mouthwateringly fine.

And she had swagger. She wore it around her like a familiar, favorite sweater. He felt his mouth fight not to smile. He liked that.

Before Sinclair had allowed him to usher her inside his office, as she'd stood framed in the doorway for a moment, he'd caught her fear. Despite the confidence, there was an undercurrent of…fear, riding her.

Hard.

His gaze swept over her, head to toe.

She nearly vibrated with energy; bravado, swag…and fear. A heady combination.

No damn way she could hide it from him. He was

the type of man that could smell it on a woman. That uncontrollable sensuality…fear. He prided himself on it being his gift.

He'd nearly pounced on her then and there. But he'd tamped his own need to conquer. *Down, boy,* he'd admonished himself. Time for that later.

She was in his camp, now.

The grin, unknown to him, broke free, tilting the corner of his mouth upward.

Nick stared. She was…tinier in real life than she appeared in photos. If he had to venture a guess, he would say she was just a few inches over five feet, which placed her more than a foot shorter than he.

His glance slid to the flashy stilettos on her small feet. Well, without those she wouldn't even make it to his chest level, he thought, frowning. Small, despite the taller-than-life heels she wore, the top of her head would barely reach him midchest without the stilettos.

As he walked behind the woman, his gaze centered on the sexy-as-hell sway of her round-but-tight butt.

So, this was Sinclair Adams. Sinclair. Sin… Yeah, that was a more apt name, he thought. She was the epitome of walking sin.

She wore a loose-fitting blouse tucked into a knee-length skirt.

Nothing overtly sexual about the outfit.

But on the woman who walked in front of him, her small hips swaying as if she *owned* the place…it was hot as hell. The skirt was a "business navy" color, as he liked to think of that particular shade of blue, yet the way it molded her hips, nipped in at the waist and curved over her rounded butt had Nick sweating as though he'd run a marathon.

She turned and he bumped into her. He reached out to steady her and realized she had come to one of the chairs in front of his desk. Realized he was holding on to her shoulders longer than what was really necessary.

But damn if he could stop himself, or remove his hands from the softness of her shoulders. Unconsciously his fingers rubbed the soft skin.

"Are you okay?" he asked. Although he knew she was, it was the best excuse he could come up with to keep his hold on her.

"Um, yeah," she said, seeming in no more of a hurry than he was to move away.

His gaze traveled over her face.

Her eyes were large and were the focal points of her heart-shaped face.

Almost too large. His gaze was stuck, as though he couldn't look away as he stared into the dark brown depths.

As he stood in front of her, so close to her, her scent drifted across his nose. Without benefit of the cracked windows or overhead swirling fan, he could *smell* her.

Damn. His nostrils flared. She had a scent unlike any he'd encountered before. Spicy and floral. A heady combination.

He forced his gaze away to take in her small nose. The small diamond chip in the crease surprised him. He cataloged that small rebellion for later contemplation.

His gaze moved on to her lips which, like her eyes, were a shade larger than would seem to work for her small face. Yet…it worked on *her*.

Full. Luscious.

The bottom lip of her perfect mouth stuck out a fraction more than the top, giving her an earthy, pouty look that had his cock pressing hard against the zipper of his jeans.

Nick had an urgent desire to grab that luscious lip and suckle it deeply into his mouth.

To see if it…she, tasted as good as both appeared to promise.

He reluctantly dragged his gaze away from her mouth to glance at her hair. Although it appeared thick, he couldn't determine the length. She had it pulled into a high bun, with soft curling tendrils hanging down her face on either side of her temples.

Something told Nick it wasn't by design that the tendrils had escaped capture. It was likely more that the strands were too damn stubborn to do as she'd instructed them to and stay confined.

Stubborn, just like the woman who had captured his attention.

The dark, soft-looking curl begged for him to reach out and touch it.

Nick felt his shaft harden. Felt the low thrum of arousal that he'd felt for her, even before he'd met the woman, sharpening, throbbing, his cock painfully erect and pressing against his zipper.

"What…what do you think you're doing?"

Her huskily asked question brought him out of his own musings. Nick's gaze caught hers and he dropped his hand.

What the hell was wrong with him? he thought. He'd been so caught up in whatever the hell was going on between them, what had been brewing between them for six months, he'd forgotten who she was.

Who he was.

He cleared his throat, motioning for her to precede him and offering her a chair that was a safe enough distance away from his desk that he could get his thoughts... and randy cock, firmly back in control.

What the hell had he been doing—thinking? He schooled his mind and wayward cock back into submission.

It was all about control.

Nick's control was legendary.

She was in his camp, now.

Yet the mocking voice inside his head whispered, reminding him how he'd felt about her, the growing feelings... After six months of foreplay—cyber foreplay—he was set to explode.

Chapter 6

Sinclair opened her briefcase, trying to still her shaky hands.

"The boys and I believe we can come to a mutually acceptable agreement, Mr. Kealoha. One I'm sure—"

"Nick."

"What?" she asked, a small frown on her face as her eyes met his, realizing he'd spoken. Damn, the man was a distraction.

"Call me Nick. I think we're past the 'Mr. Kealoha' stage, don't you?" he asked, and she found herself staring at his strong fingers as he poured coffee into a mug, then handed the mug to her.

Immediately after the odd yet sexually disturbing first introduction, she wasn't sure what she expected to happen.

Would he come on to her now? Was it all part of some weird game to undermine what she'd come here to do? To set her up so that she'd forget the purpose of the visit?

If so, he had another think coming. She was back in control and nothing, absolutely nothing, was going to make her lose it. It was not going to happen.

"And I'm assuming you mean you and the Wildes?"

She glanced at him, her gaze sharp. She frowned. "Of course the Wildes. Who else?"

He leaned back in the oversize desk chair. Despite the largeness of the leather chair, he still dominated it, as she would imagine he dominated any room, any place he was.

He was *just* that kind of man.

His lips were curled into a ghost of a smile.

She felt a shudder run through her body and suppressed it.

Business at hand.

If she continued to have to remind herself of *that* simple little fact…she was in a world of trouble.

A look passed across his handsome face. One which she couldn't determine the exact meaning of.

"Well…as you referred to them collectively as 'the boys,' I assumed you meant the Wildes. Or do you represent another group of *lost* boys?" he asked sardonically, one dark eyebrow raised in question.

Sinclair sat straighter in her chair, frowning, keeping his gaze.

She opened her mouth to snap out a retort before closing it, her mind going back over her words. She looked away from him.

She bit back a sigh of embarrassment and barely refrained from slumping back against the soft leather seat. He was right. Damn it.

She had referred to them as *the boys*. She silenced a groan of embarrassment.

Having grown up around the brothers, men who were like older brothers to Sinclair when she was a child, she had always referred to them in that manner as had some others in the small community in Wyoming. Although most people now just called them the Wildes, she, and a select few others, had the liberty of long association with the men and continued to refer to them collectively in that manner.

But Sinclair had never used the nickname for the men while conducting business. Particularly when the business she was conducting was on the Wildes' behalf.

Nicholas Kealoha had her so rattled that she'd slipped up and done something she never had before.

Control. She fought hard to bring it back.

She plastered a smile on her face and observed him. Just as he'd made the comment, she'd caught the look on his face. She hadn't missed his "Neverland" reference.

Sinclair decided to keep the peace and not call him out on his attempted slam. Calling three men who were the antithesis to Peter Pan's Lost Boys was a ridiculous insult and one she refused to even acknowledge…while praying to heaven that somehow the men hadn't developed ESP. Her Wildes were true alpha men, the kind of men one did not mess with, as her father had once put it, just not in such mild language.

Yet for as rugged and alpha as the Wildes were, Sinclair would hate to see any of them go toe-to-toe with *this* man.

Her glance stole over him.

He smiled slightly at her, one corner of his sensual mouth hitching up ever so slightly.

In that way he had....

The way that made her wish some resourceful designer had invented air-conditioned panties.

Damn, he was hot.

He took up way too much...space. She was hot. Damn, it was hot. She resisted the urge to retrieve a slip of loose paper from her briefcase to fan herself. Besides, the place she really needed to fan, she couldn't. She felt a blush steal across her face.

A knowing look passed in his aquamarine blue eyes, and the blush intensified.

Before she'd met Nick, Sinclair had never thought she'd meet another man who could come close to the Wildes in sheer masculinity.

She turned her attention away from Nick to the business at hand.

"Well, I'd like to start an initial dialogue on what the Wildes are offering, and we can go from there in the negotiations. I think you and your family will agree that it is a fair deal," she began. In control.

She deftly unclasped the hook of her chic custom-made briefcase, a gift from the Wildes upon graduating from law school.

She withdrew an e-tablet from inside and automatically removed the clamp, attaching it to the leather handles of her briefcase before hooking it to the arm of the chair.

She caught his look. She didn't feel the need to explain why she didn't want her bag on the floor.

"As I was saying, the Wildes have come to an agreement, and the proposal they have given me permission to offer you and your family is more than fair, we all believe," she stated clearly, redirecting the energy away from the direction it had been headed.

She had no intention of being at the Kealoha ranch, or in Hawaii for that matter, for longer than was absolutely necessary. Although Nate and the family had given her carte blanche in the way of time, telling her to take the time she needed to take care of the matter, she planned to be as speedy about the business as possible. Thorough, without a doubt, but with a quickness.

She handed the e-tablet over to him, ignoring the snap of electricity that zinged back and forth the minute their fingertips touched.

The ghost of a smile remained on his face as he took the tablet from her hands.

She kept her face neutral and after long moments he sat back in the oversize chair and finally released her from his stare.

Sinclair resisted the urge to wipe away the bead of sweat she felt running down the back of her neck. She also stopped herself from slumping against the cool leather chair; she continued to wonder if it was hot in his office or if it was just her.

Control.

Throughout the meeting, Nick sat back and listened to her, allowing nothing of what he felt, nothing of what he was even *thinking,* to show on his face.

With Sinclair, he had ascertained that beyond the beautiful face, the hot-as-hell voice and body made for sex, she was a force to be reckoned with. Intelligence and confidence fairly vibrated from her small sexy body.

Her sensuality was one he found intriguing; so far, he'd figured out that she allowed only tiny snapshots of it to the world.

The small nuances told him she was not the conservative button-down corporate attorney that she presented to the world, from the small diamond chip in her nose, to the matching pink-tipped manicured nails and toes, which he'd caught a glimpse of from the peep-toe high-heeled shoes she wore. She tried to hide her sensuality. But it was there.

Hell, her curves alone told that story.

Sexy, with an edge.

Earthy, yet restrained.

As she'd outlined the proposal from the Wildes, she'd pulled out numerous documents. He'd noticed that they were all in order, filed in an accordion-style folder, and mirrored what he was reading on the tablet she'd handed him.

Prim and proper. With hidden fire.

He had to force himself to listen, to concentrate on what she was saying. He knew that a lot was riding on the situation, but damn if she hadn't made it nearly impossible for him to maintain focus.

However, her next words caught his attention, snapping him sharply back to the present and the situation at hand.

"So we, the Wildes, feel this unpleasant situation can be remedied to all parties' satisfaction. In exchange for you and your brother signing the document, we will withdraw all charges against you."

He heard and swiftly cataloged what she'd said. But it was one word...one phrase that caught his attention beyond the rest.

Unpleasant situation.

That, and charges against them.

Renewed bitterness toward the man who was his and Key's biological father rose swiftly. He shoved the emotions—anger, resentment—down, and focused on the rest of what she was saying. Focused on what was really important. None of the rest mattered.

He ignored the pang in his heart at the cavalier dismissal of his and his brother's importance in the Wildes' eyes.

His jaw tightened.

"Hold on," he snapped, holding up a hand for her to stop speaking. He glanced at her quickly and saw that his gesture didn't sit well with her.

Good. Because her dismissal of him and his brother didn't sit well with him, either.

He took his time as he scanned the last page of the document. And then, although he'd caught the gist of it, he swiped a finger over the tablet screen to take it back to the previous page to reread.

He frowned.

"Exactly what charges are you talking about for my brother and me to drop?"

She sat back and gave him a *look,* withdrawing the half-glasses she'd perched upon the narrow bridge of her nose.

"Mr. Kealoha, have you not been paying attention to what I've been saying? What I've been proposing for you and for your family?"

Nick wasn't easily embarrassed. Yet at that moment he was, and the feeling ticked him off. He was irritated not with her but with himself for so easily allowing her to distract him.

He stared across the expanse of the desk at Sinclair Adams.

She smiled.

His eyes narrowed. He'd have to watch her. Her hold on him was one that he wouldn't tolerate. It had been… interesting, before he'd met her. The way he'd think about her, allow her to filter into his thoughts at night, mostly, when he was relaxing, and moments before succumbing to sleep. But that was as far as it was going to go, as far as he would allow it to go.

Damn. He needed his full attention on this matter. He

sat straighter in his chair, making subtle readjustments against his randy cock inside his jeans.

"Never had a problem with my concentration, Ms. Adams. Everything I do…" he drawled, keeping his gaze on her. "I do with extreme focus. Ma'am," he finished. And smiled at her.

He caught the way her light brown cheeks blushed fiery red at his words.

Good. Score one for Team Kealoha. Control was back in his corner.

Now that he had it, he knew he had to put his cock, and what he wanted to do to her with it, away for the moment to truly concentrate on what she was saying and what the damn Wildes were proposing.

"In layman's terms, the charge you and your family have levied against the Wildes claiming right of inheritance. We are simply proposing that, as the late Clint Jedediah Wilde had no knowledge of you or your brother, it was without malice that you and your brother were not included in the inheritance of his property as well as monetary inheritance. Because of this, your lawsuit is, in fact, unwarranted. However, we are willing to discuss a settlement."

"A settlement, huh?" he said, feelings of anger swamping him as well as his judgment. Making him completely put to the side that he had actually decided not to go forward with the lawsuit. "I'm not sure this… proposal is going to work."

"And your brother? Your father? What are their thoughts on this situation? Do they share your feelings?"

she asked, pinning him with a look. "And don't you have to show this to them first? To your brother?"

He felt the heat of her focused stare.

Discerning.

It was as though she saw right through him. He'd been right in his assessment of her: she was one to watch. He'd have to make sure at all times that he was the one in the driver's seat; he could tell she was used to that privilege belonging to her.

He subtly adjusted his approach.

"Of course I do. And I will, Ms. Sinclair. We are a united family," he said, deftly sidestepping the question.

She stared at him, not saying a word, simply holding his gaze.

She finally spoke. "That wasn't exactly what I asked, Mr. Kealoha."

He knew what she was asking. He simply had no intention of answering. Not until he had a hold on the situation and had decided exactly what he *did* want and how he planned to go about seducing her out of it.

His initial anger gone, he had been ready to tell the Wildes and their attorney to go to hell. But now, all of that had changed. Now he wanted to…play…with the Wildes' attorney.

"Just like the Wildes, the Kealohas are united." His mouth firmed briefly before relaxing, a smile crossing his wide lips. "In fact, in the spirit of the Hawaiian tradition of welcome, why don't you meet them? My family, that is," he said when she looked confused. "Tonight."

Before she could protest, he finished, "Have dinner with me." He smiled at the look of surprise on her face. "With my family."

Chapter 7

Have dinner with me.

The request caught her off guard and Sinclair tilted her head to the side. "For what purpose? I think you've made your position clear. And to that end, I think it best for me to wait for you to confer with your family before we go further, Mr. Kealoha."

The entire time she'd been in the meeting with him, her nerves had been taut, tighter than a string on one of her guitars.

The fact that she'd managed to speak in an intelligent manner was something she was eternally grateful for. The man had her on *edge*...

She struggled to clear her head. She couldn't say it was anything he was doing; couldn't really pin any one thing, one action or word that put her in the state she was in.

Nothing other than him.

She sucked in a breath, her glance stealing over his hard body. And he was enough.

She kept her attention on the estate matter, reminding herself of her years of concentrating on long, boring legal briefs that no matter how mind-numbing, she had to plough through to not only understand but to pass her exams.

"We can discuss this further. Nothing is set in stone, Ms. Adams. Besides, I need to speak to my brother, and sister-in-law, and of course my father, before going any further. It is, and will be, a family decision." For a moment a hard look crossed his handsome face and she felt her heart thump against her chest in reaction.

In that moment she saw how he and his brother, along with their father had one of the most prosperous ranches in Hawaii. Just like her Wildes, this man and his family were a force to be reckoned with.

But so was she.

She offered a broad smile.

"I think our work is concluded for now, Mr. Kealoha," Sinclair said, closing the fastener on her briefcase and preparing to leave. "If you could contact me once you have presented the proposal to your family, I would appreciate it. Although you have my cell, here is my card. On the back I have the hotel name and number where I can be reached," she said, withdrawing a card from her wallet and placing it on his desk.

He lifted it, examining the card, turning it over, his brow furrowed.

She had to get out of there. Now. She needed to collect her thoughts, set up a game plan.

The meeting had begun with a rocky start, yet over the course of the past hour and a half, it had gotten smoother and she'd relaxed. As much as one could relax with a predator in the room. One that looked ready to pounce at any moment, despite the relaxed manner he'd showed throughout the meeting. Sinclair shuddered.

Yet for all of that, Sinclair felt as though she'd been in a battle with a tsunami.

And she wasn't sure she'd been the victor. Unlike most times in her interactions and in her role as an attorney, when she'd felt sure, confident. Yes, she felt confident in her abilities as a damn good attorney and in her negotiation abilities.

She'd stolen a glance at him from beneath lowered lids on more than one occasion throughout the time of the meeting. The last time he'd caught her, she'd glanced away, pretending a nonchalance she felt anything but.

The entire time she'd tried to ignore the strong attraction she felt for him. Yet her glance would steal over his strong arms, braced on the armrests of his chair, and the soft-looking chambray shirt that lay open at the top, exposing a black, V-necked T-shirt stretched over a hard-muscled, broad chest. Not to mention the faded Levi's covering long legs stretched out in front of him or the large, cowboy-boot-clad feet casually crossed at the ankles beneath the desk.

Her gaze caught on the lean planes of his face, the intensity of his blue eyes, deep set and heavily rimmed by thick dark lashes. The lashes being so dark against his blue eyes, coupled with the way she'd catch him eyeing her, had been unsettling. Intense. It was as though he was looking at her and had discerned her deepest, most…private thoughts.

A tiny shiver feathered down her spine.

It was her ability to withstand him as a woman that she was concerned about.

Quickly she stood and, with nervous hands, clutched her briefcase closer to her body, as though it could ward him off.

"Staying at the Royale, huh?" he asked.

She felt as though he were mocking her somehow.

"Yes. The Wildes made the reservations," she murmured.

"Nothing but the best for their…lawyer," he said, and she felt her hackles rise.

Yes, it was a luxury hotel, with a spa, as well.

After Althea Wilde had made the reservations and Sinclair realized how luxurious the hotel was, she'd protested, to which Althea had hushed her and laughed.

"Girl, you may as well enjoy Hawaii while you're there. No sense otherwise! Besides, Nate agreed with me when I told him," she'd said with a wink.

Reluctantly, Sinclair had accepted the grand gesture. She knew that Althea had grown up with money as the only child in a wealthy political family, though she herself had had to work hard at minimum-wage jobs from mechanic to waitress for a stretch of time as she had been on the run from a crazed ex-lover before coming to the Wilde Ranch.

"Yes, well, as I said, there is my contact information," was the only thing she said in reply.

He stood, as well. She gulped down a breath as she gazed over at him. Unable to move, but knowing she should, she stood rooted to the spot, transfixed.

He kept her gaze.

Feet, move, damn it!

Nothing. She couldn't move an inch to save her life. She finally was able to stop gawking at the man and breathed a sigh of relief. She turned to pick up her purse and looped it over her shoulder before turning to face him.

"Beautiful." His deep, sexy voice said the word with an almost…reverent sound.

Startled, Sinclair met his gaze, her heartbeat racing at the compliment.

"The leather," he continued. "It's gorgeous. May I?" he asked.

Before Sinclair could respond yes or no, much less acknowledge the ridiculous disappointing feeling that he wasn't referring to her but her briefcase, he strode over to her.

He reached out and touched the soft case, running his fingers over the supple leather.

"Um…yes," Sinclair sputtered, caught off guard. "I suppose it is," she finished, unnerved by the interaction. "Okay, that is. For you to touch my briefcase."

She stopped speaking, feeling all kinds of crazy.

Instead of his eyes on her, he was staring at her briefcase. She didn't know if she should be insulted or not, she thought, a strange need to laugh coming over her.

His glance met hers, a wicked grin on his face.

"Soft, supple…smooth," he said, his voice lowering. "I like things… smooth."

As she watched him fingering her briefcase, her breath caught in her throat.

She moistened her lower lip. "Thank you," she replied, her voice low. "I think," she mumbled before lifting her eyes to his. She cleared her throat. "It was a graduation gift," she said and watched again as his fingers reached out and caressed the leather.

Her gaze was caught on the action.

His fingers—long, strong and masculine. Just like the rest of him. As she stared in hapless fascination as his able fingers caressed the leather of her briefcase, she found herself wanting, for a brief moment, to feel his fingers doing the same thing to her skin.

She swallowed the melon-ball-size lump that had formed at the back of her throat at the thought.

"Let me guess… Your *Wilde Boys* gave it to you?"

The statement barely registered, yet she nodded.

"Yes. A gift. For graduating," she said again and felt foolish for unknown reasons. Now, besides the breathless quality, she knew she didn't exactly sound like the Rhodes scholar she in fact had been.

The man was reducing her to a mumbling simpleton.

"Why don't you come to dinner with me...I mean, the family, Ms. Sinclair? What do you have to be afraid of?" he asked.

It took more than a moment for her to switch gears, snatch her mind from where it was headed to focus on the question.

"What do you have to be afraid of?" he repeated.

Her focus went to his sensual mouth.

A challenge.

He was issuing a challenge. One she knew if she were the smart woman she always prided herself on being, she would definitely ignore. Any business they conducted could be during regular business hours. End of subject.

She dragged her attention away from his strong fingers, and the way he was absently working the leather of her case.

Her gaze met his.

Yes, in them she saw the challenge. She also saw the look of something else in their deep blue depths. Something that was immediately shut down before she could truly see.

"What time?" she asked.

Obviously that something else she'd seen, or thought she'd seen, made her throw caution...and no doubt common sense, right on out the window.

A slow grin tugged the corners of his mouth up into a

grin that promised he was absolutely the bad-boy player she'd thought he was from the first moment she'd laid eyes on his image.

Chapter 8

"Have dinner with me. The family, that is."

The request was out of his mouth before he could retract the offer, not that he would want to.

Nick had read the surprise in her face, one that spoke volumes.

Had he not been experiencing that disquieting feeling that told him he was in trouble—deep-shit trouble—in the form of the petite, sexy woman who'd stood in front of him, he might have retracted his words.

Or *because* that same feeling, if he were a sane man, would have made him rethink the invitation.

What the hell had he been thinking, anyway?

Nick ran the brush over the horse's silky coat, his mind on the meeting he'd had the previous day with Sinclair Adams.

When she'd agreed, he'd known it was pride that had her doing so; she hadn't wanted to show any weakness. Which was what he'd been counting on. He'd known because, instinctively, he felt she was his kindred spirit in that vein; had the shoe been on the other foot, he would have done the same.

Then his glance had run over her face. The sharpness of her eyes had struck him, the slight shadows beneath them a testimony to her exhaustion.

At first he'd been prepared to try to ignore her look of fragility. A fragility he knew without having been told was one she tried to keep hidden. With a clarity that came from out of nowhere, Nick knew that for all the projection of confident lawyer—which he knew her to be—she was beyond exhausted.

And when she'd told him about the car breaking down, he'd admittedly felt a stab of guilt. It had been childish of him to send Kanoa. He'd known the elderly man's vehicle, as much as he loved it, was unreliable at best. Nick had told himself, tried to convince himself, that he'd sent Kanoa out there simply to throw some business the older man's way. But that was a lie. Between him and his brother, they usually kept the elderly man "busy" with work: odd-end jobs around the ranch that didn't require much in the way of labor.

He should have had one of the guys from the ranch go out to get her— Hell, he should have done it himself.

Nick refused to acknowledge, even to himself, that there was any reason beyond being too busy to do so himself.

He continued running the brush over the mare, his thoughts pensive.

In the end he'd retracted the offer, claiming that he'd forgotten an engagement he'd already agreed to, and promptly hid a masculine grin at the knowing look that crossed her beautiful face.

The fact that she'd thought his "previous engagement" was a date was easy to discern from her expression before she'd shut it down.

The fact that it had…upset her had been visible in her dark brown eyes, as well, before she'd shuttered her lids, lowering them as she fiddled with the clasp on her bag.

He'd felt an odd catch in his chest at the small action. She'd looked so vulnerable….

From the moment their eyes had met, Nick had been like a damn fish out of water.

With a sigh, Nick began to water down the horse, his thoughts on the woman he knew was going to be more trouble than he'd originally thought.

And all because he couldn't stop thinking about her. She'd invaded his dreams; months ago, before he'd even met her. Sinclair had done that. Her hold on him was one he didn't understand, and a big part of him damn sure didn't like it. It was…uncomfortable. New.

He'd never thought of a woman nonstop, in the way he thought of her, and it had nothing to do with the Kealoha ranch or the Wildes and the Wyoming Wilde Ranch.

Damn the Wildes *and* their ranch; he didn't want anything to do with them, or it. It was all her. Sinclair.

What had started as a way to get back at the Wildes

was now something more. He wanted her to stay around for a while…to get her out of his system, to get her out of his thoughts.

And although he had no intention of pursuing the Wildes' inheritance, he had to make her think that he did. To that end Nick knew he needed his family's help, even if they didn't know they were helping him, or for what reason. They needed to go along with him. Be the united front he'd claimed them to be.

Oh, yeah, and added to that…Key needed to bring his new wife into the deception, as well. Just to make it more convincing. Yeah, that was going to be a lot of fun, he thought, convincing his twin of *that*.

Just as that thought came along, Sonia walked inside the stable, along with the horse her husband had recently purchased for her at auction.

He grinned, his mood improving.

He knew Sonia had a soft spot for him, as he had been rooting for her and his brother during their courtship as well as their breakup. He liked to think he was the reason his knuckle-headed brother had seen the light and hadn't allowed the best thing to ever happen to him walk away.

He hadn't cashed in on his favor…yet.

Sonia had gone out of town yesterday on a short trip to the main island to meet with one of the investors for the new show she was producing. He had to get to her now, convince her to help him out, before Key knew what hit him.

He felt suddenly like rubbing his hands together like a cheesy villain in a badly produced horror flick.

"Hey, you! When did you get back in town?" he asked, as though he hadn't been aware she was in the stable. He gave his own mare a final wipe down before closing and locking the horse's stall.

He threw Sonia a grin, casually, as he quickly strode to her side.

"Let me help you with that," Nick said, hustling to reach her in time to take the horse's reins from Sonia's surprised grasp.

She tilted her head to the side and stared up at him, a question on her pretty face.

"What? Can't a man help his favorite sister-in-law out?" he asked.

"Favorite sister-in-law, huh?" Sonia replied. One hand on her hip in question. "How about *only* sister-in-law?" she asked with a laugh, but allowed him to take the reins. As she followed him to the horse's stall, he felt her eyes on his back the entire time.

He knew he had about as much chance of getting something sneaky past Sonia as he did his brother: nil to no chance at all.

But unlike his brother, with Sonia he stood a chance of leaning, heavily, on the whole "you owe me" thing he had going.

As far as using the guilt trip for his brother... He wanted to save that one. For the time he *really* needed to call in a favor.

Not that he thought she truly *did* owe him for the coming together of her and his brother. He knew that eventually the two would have done so, with or without his help.

"So what's up, brother-in-law? What do you want? Want to meet one of the interns I just hired? Listen, after that last fiasco where we had to call the police, I prefer we keep business and personal separate!"

"No! I don't want to meet your intern!" he railed as he began to lead the horse away. "It's nothing like that. Geesh, does it always have to be me wanting to meet a woman, for me to want to help my sister-in-law out?"

Sonia gave him a look.

He swore.

"You know you're becoming more and more like my brother every day!" he complained as he led her horse inside its stall.

She laughed and went over to grab the feed for the horse as Nick began to rub it down.

"Sorry, Pika" she said, smiling affectionately at the faux look of offense on his handsome face. "Okay. Thank you for the help. I was wrong. You're sweet as pie. And so generous. And helpful… Did I mention helpful?" she asked, holding back a laugh.

The jig was up. She knew he wanted something from her. Hell, he might as well get on with it.

"Okay, here it is," he began, pausing slightly when he heard her choke back a laugh. "I want you to help me convince Key to attend a family dinner."

She frowned as she brought the feed pail over to her mare.

"What's so hard about that? That's cake. We eat dinner as a family all the time! And now with Dad out of the hospital and almost back to a hundred percent, family dinners are a regular thing. Which I love! In fact, I was thinking of asking Mahi to make me some of his delicious—"

"Sonia, wait a minute!" he broke in, laughing and shaking his head at his sister-in–law's enthusiasm for Mahi's cooking…and family. For a moment the smile lingered on his face as he glanced over at her and her face lit up. "I wasn't talking about just the immediate family. I was thinking more along the lines of inviting someone—" He stopped, inhaled. Finished, "A woman."

And waited for it. *It* being her reaction.

He didn't have long to wait.

Sonia spun around so fast on her booted feet she nearly did a three-sixty, her spin worthy of making any prima ballerina envious.

He snickered but leaped to where she stood, reaching out a hand to steady her on her feet.

"I'll take this!" he said, taking the pail of feed from her hands and hooking it on to the attachment on the wall.

He gently swatted her mare's rear end, encouraging it to go and eat.

"Okay. Now back it up, mister. Wh-what? You? Invite someone to dinner… A *woman?*" she asked, astonishment on her gamine face.

"Don't act so surprised. I don't know if I should be offended by your shock," he said, walking over to the supplies they kept nearby, grabbing a brush and returning. He began stroking it over the mare, but gave up the brush to Sonia when she held out her hand.

"Okay. Spill," she demanded.

She began to brush the animal, pleasure in her face as she took over the task. Nick leaned against the stall wall and crossed his arms over his chest.

She had taken to ranch life as though she'd been born to it. From the moment she'd set foot on the ranch he'd known she was destined to stay.

From the moment she and his brother had first laid eyes on each other, fireworks erupted and *everyone* had known she was there to stay.

He shook his head at his own sentimental thoughts, laughing at himself.

None of that was for him—the destined-mate thing. Immediately, Sinclair's image appeared in his mind.

Sonia chose that moment to glance at him over her shoulder as she continued to brush the mare.

She gasped, her mouth forming a perfect *O*.

"Oooh…. You're thinking about her now!"

Despite himself, he chuckled. "You know…you sounded like a little kid when you just said that, right?"

"I may sound like a little kid, but Pika has a *girrrrl-friend*. Pika has a *girrrrlfriend*." She giggled, further making her point, then laughed outright when he reached down to the floor, grabbed a fistful of hay and tossed it at her.

"Brat," he said good-naturedly.

She brushed aside the hay in her hair, laughing, "I just got my hair done, boy!"

He laughed along with her, thinking that only Sonia could get away with calling him *boy*.

Looking at his sister-in-law's hair that lay on her shoulders, unpinned, as well as the casual way she disregarded the hay, made him think of Sinclair.

He wondered if she ever let her hair down. Just completely relaxed, and allowed herself to be free like that. He knew she had it in her to do so.

He did a quick reality check, and admitted to himself that just about everything reminded him of the woman.

"It's Sinclair Adams," he said and carefully watched his sister-in-law's reaction.

She went back to the task of brushing the mare's rich dark coat, her expression sobering. "Oh…I see. Was she here, then?" she asked, knowing that the lawyer had been expected to visit the ranch.

He was counting on the fact that his brother hadn't informed his wife of all the details, and the fact that he'd given Nick the responsibility for "dealing with" Sinclair, as Key had put it.

He scratched his head, suddenly ill at ease. He'd have to tread carefully.

"She is. And thing is, I'm not all that sure what I think about it all."

"In what way?"

He sighed. "It's no secret how I felt about my mother and…Clint Wilde. The whole secrecy behind who our father was…. Why our parents never told us…" he began.

Sonya nodded, yet remained silent.

She, like Key and their father, as well as those other

few close members of their extended family, was aware of Nick's anger over the deception.

"What I do know is that I invited her here with the intention of getting what I thought my brother and I were due. I own up to that. But now that she's here... Hell, Sonia, I'm just not sure."

"Do you still feel that way, Pika? That the Wildes... owe you?"

"Not so much 'owe' as I guess I just wanted an explanation."

"For?" she asked, continuing to brush the animal, giving it her attention.

Yet Nick knew she was giving closer attention to what he was telling her. It wasn't every day that Nick opened up.

"For?" he asked, anger tightening his face. "For...why the hell Clint Wilde never checked up on Mom after she left. All this love he had for her... Why not check up on her to make sure she was okay?" he snapped.

She turned to look at him. The softening of her expression and the sympathy he saw there was something he didn't want.

Even from his sister-in-law, whom he loved; he did not want her to feel sorry for him.

His face hardened.

"Pika..."

He glanced down to see her hand on his arm. He hadn't even been aware that she had moved toward him.

He barely refrained from shrugging her off, instead forcing the frown he knew was on his face away and his muscles to loosen. He was so tense he felt an ache in his shoulders where his muscles had bunched.

"Hey, it's not a big deal. I'm a big boy. I'm good." He shrugged off the anger…the unresolved feelings he felt for a man long dead. "But now that she's here, I want her to know that my family is united. I want her to meet the family. If for no other reason than to let the Wildes know we are united."

"Are you sure it's her you want to know this?"

He pinned her with a glare. "I don't need a pop-therapy session, Sonia." He'd hurled the words and felt guilty when her eyes widened and her mouth turned down at the corners.

"I know, Pika… I'm sorry," she said as he reached over and gave her a quick impromptu hug.

"You didn't do anything, Sonia. It's me." He laughed without humor. "Just trying to figure all of this out. Figured us coming together, showing unity, would send a message, I guess." He rubbed the back of his neck in an unconscious gesture he and his brother shared when they were uncertain.

Sonia recognized the gesture and her face softened even more.

"That's pretty important to you, isn't it? The family showing unity?"

"Yeah," he said, turning to put away the supplies. There was a short silence before Sonia spoke.

"Well, that's good enough for me. What can I do to help? And, yes, Pika…I know that my husband put this ball in your court," she said.

He turned to face her, surprised.

She shrugged. "Doesn't mean I can't—or won't—help my favorite brother-in-law out," she said, volleying back his earlier words with a spin. "So…what's the plan?"

He glanced at Sonia as she rubbed her hands together, preparing to plot like that cheesy villain in a badly produced horror flick he'd thought of earlier.

He laughed outright.

Chapter 9

Nick was unlike anyone that Sinclair had ever met.

After the dinner with his family the night before, a few days after her arrival at the ranch, he was more of an enigma than ever to Sinclair.

She'd been glad for the reprieve; instead of facing his family that same horrendous day of her arrival, she'd been able to take a few days, acclimate to the time change as well as relax a bit.

She'd gone back to her room, unpacked and gotten herself "comfortable." She was a self-proclaimed "neat freak," preferring things be put in an orderly fashion.

It came from a lifetime of living in smaller quarters. She and her father had lived in one of the guest cottages on the Wilde Ranch, as many of the families had, and although the cottage was nicely kept—quaint—it hadn't been large. However, it had been enough room for the two of them.

Dorm life and a series of smaller studios and apartments had strengthened her habits. So, after making sure she'd put everything in its place, she'd also set up all of her gadgets: laptop, iPad, iPad mini and iPhone. She was a self-proclaimed gadget junkie.

Then she'd promptly fallen asleep after taking a long hot shower. The last thought on her mind: Nick Kealoha.

After waking up the next day, refreshed, she'd called the ranch. When Ellie Wilde had answered, she'd smiled. Sinclair loved all of the Wilde women. Each woman was unique, with her own very distinct personality, and they were all very loving women.

Yet, of all the Wilde women, she identified with Ellie the most.

Studious and serious, Ellie, too, had grown up around the ranch. Although she hadn't actually lived on the ranch, as she and Yasmine Wilde had, Ellie knew ranch life just as well, if not more. Her father had been the veterinarian for the Wilde Ranch and Ellie had followed in his footsteps.

The reason Sinclair identified with Ellie just a little more than Yasmine was that in addition to being an academic, as Sinclair had been, Ellie tended to be quiet, and had also grown up with only her father as a parent.

She smiled, now, as she took out a mug from the small overhead cabinet and poured herself a cup of the coffee she'd brewed. Taking it, she sat at the small table in the kitchenette of her suite and recalled their earlier phone conversation.

"Hi, ladybug, how's it going?" Ellie had asked in her low-toned, melodic voice.

"It's going!" she'd said, grimacing.

She'd laughed when Ellie replied, "Oh, Lord...what's happened so far? That didn't sound so good!"

She'd briefly retold what had happened to her during her trip so far, making light of the entire thing. As well as glossing over the effect Nick Kealoha seemed to have on her. She was close to the Wilde women, but not ready to disclose how she felt about Nickolas Kealoha.

She herself wasn't even sure how she felt.

"And how's it going with Nick Kealoha?"

The direct question had made her tense. Had Ellie somehow known about her odd relationship with the Kealoha?

"Nate mentioned that he was your point of contact? Or are you dealing with the other brother...Keanu?"

She'd felt her body relax. Ellie hadn't known. Sinclair had briefed her on what had occurred, and asked Ellie to relay the message to the Wilde men that she'd met with the Kealohas and everything was on task.

After that, she'd caught up on ranch life with Ellie. She'd smiled and given her loving congratulations when Ellie told her that she and Shilah recently found out they were pregnant.

"How is he taking it?" Sinclair had asked, a grin on her face as she'd pictured Ellie's husband watching her every move. Just as his brothers were when it came to their women, Shilah Wilde was fiercely protective of Ellie. Although she had a practice in the city, seeing domesticated animals of the town near their ranch, Ellie was not only the vet for the Wilde Ranch but would also lend a hand when needed on the smaller ranches nearby. The work could be hard and grueling, particularly when it was a difficult birth for one of the larger animals.

Because of this, Shilah tended to...worry about her. And that was putting it mildly. The man was crazy about his wife, she knew, which seemed to be a running theme with the Wildes.

Even before learning of the pregnancy, he would go with her when he could to help her in her practice, particularly when her father or one of her assistants was unable.

"Oh, my goodness...don't get me started," she had said with a wry laugh. "Now what do you *think,* Sinclair?" Ellie'd then asked, sounding exasperated. But Sinclair knew that the woman loved every minute of her husband's overprotective ways. The Wilde men were alpha men; no two ways about it, they protected what they considered theirs.

"I can only imagine." She'd laughed along with Ellie and listened as she'd filled her in on the other happenings on the ranch.

Sinclair sat back in the chair and finished her coffee, the smile on her face slowly dropping as she thought back over the dinner she'd had with the Kealohas and what she *hadn't* told Ellie.

* * *

Not knowing what to expect, Sinclair dressed carefully for her meeting with the Kealohas. Although he'd made it seem as though it were just a friendly meet-and-greet dinner at the ranch, in her mind, Sinclair firmly placed it in the business-only category.

It was bad enough she was having a difficult time separating business from pleasure with Nick, thinking not only of their six-month-long…foreplay, she thought, blushing, but of their over-the-top explosive first meeting, as well.

She still blushed thinking of their first meeting earlier that week. The way he'd been instrumental in taking feelings that she'd already begun to sense—feelings she didn't want to name—to the nth degree, turning her on, making her sweat…making her wet.

She ran her hands over her hair.

She'd spent the past few days learning as much about the Kealohas and their ranch as she could, all low key, not asking overt questions of anyone, just casual questions, as though she were another tourist. Her objective: knowing who she was dealing with from a different vantage point.

Which wasn't difficult; everyone knew the Kealohas, both the locals as well as the tourists. She'd learned more than she'd wanted to while on a tourist shuttle and listening to the two young ladies giggling in front of her. Twins, from the looks of them, they spoke loud enough for anyone to hear about how they were going to meet the "dynamic duo" and what they were going to do to them once they did.

Sinclair prided herself on being a grown woman, confident and accomplished.

Although somewhat inexperienced, she still thought herself to be sophisticated and aware…but after listening to the young women, she didn't know the last time she'd blushed and been more uncomfortable…yet strangely intrigued. Were some of the things they'd said even humanly possible to perform? she wondered.

Besides her encounter with the amorous twins, exploring the island the Kealohas' A'kela Ranch was located on had been an eye-opener for Sinclair. She had seen for herself the amazing impact their ranch had on their community as one of the most profitable family-owned ranches in all of Hawaii.

She'd gone into one of the local shops and listened as the owner had been on the phone with someone from the Kealoha ranch. After hanging up, there'd been a relieved smile on the woman's aged, dusky face. "Thank God for the Kealohas," she'd said and smiled at Sinclair.

"Something good happen?" Sinclair had boldly asked, yet kept her voice and question light.

"My grandson attends the University of Hawaii," she'd said, gathering Sinclair's small items and preparing to ring them up. "Money was getting tighter, and the Aloha Keiki Foundation is going to pick up the tab for his senior year!" she'd told her, a wide smile on her brown, leathery face.

Sinclair had smiled and congratulated the woman, yet

she'd been bothered by the idea that she had been wrong about the Kealohas. A pensive mood engulfed her for the rest of the day, as she'd toured the small town and learned of other small ways the Kealohas impacted the community they lived in.

She arrived at the family's sprawling ranch home on time and ready. She'd brought everything with her, armed herself with her beloved electronic gadgets as well as the documents she'd again gone over to make sure she'd covered all of the facts Nick had made bullet points about. She was ready for the family meeting with her guard up, ready to defend her Wildes *if* and *when* the opportunity arose.

Surprisingly, as the night wore on, the need for a swift defense would never come up.

She was greeted at the door by the housekeeper, who she learned was known simply as Mahi. Although concise in manner and speech, she felt the warmth in his welcome of her into their home.

She smiled at his demeanor. It reminded her keenly of Mama Lilly, the woman who had been the housekeeper for the Wildes from the time Clint Jedediah Wilde had bought the ranch. Like Lilly, Mahi's easy manner was one that instantly put her at ease.

And if she'd thought Mahi had been a fluke, she'd been mistaken, quickly.

"Come in, come in! You must be Ms. Adams. So nice to meet you. I'm Sonia Kealoha!" No sooner had she been ushered into the large, majestic-looking foyer, than a beautiful woman was headed her way, hand out-stretched. Close behind her was a man Sinclair knew had to be Nick's identical twin, Keanu Kealoha.

Forcing a smile on her face, and telling her feet to move forward, she placed a hand within the woman's and shook it, her grip firm.

"Mrs. Kealoha, it's nice to meet you," she said, keeping a pleasant expression on her face. "I saw the new documentary on ranching and the impact on the environment from a naturalist point of view that you directed a few months ago on the network. Very impressive."

The woman's eyes widened fractionally before the smile blossomed even more.

"Why, thank you so much. That means a lot! It's a new venture of mine, producing documentaries. It's been quite a change from my normal undertakings. A little scary, but hey, change is good." She stopped and smiled, her cheeks dimpling as she did. With a shrug she continued, "And not only did I direct it, I produced it," she said, and Sinclair caught the way her husband's hand tightened more on her waist and the pride in his blue eyes as he glanced at his wife as she spoke. "I'm very proud of the reception it has been receiving. I'm so happy you enjoyed it!"

"I did, very much. I rarely have time for television, but when I saw the reviews of your documentary, it was something I knew I couldn't miss. And I was right. It was brilliant!"

Everything she said was true. The documentary had

been riveting, and unlike many documentaries on the environment, it had been vibrant and at times even funny.

Sonia Kealoha was eating up the compliments with a big smile on her face. It didn't hurt Sinclair in her end game; *keep the enemy off guard.*

"And as I'm sure you know, this is my husband, Key…Keanu, that is," she said as the man came closer. He stuck out a hand for her to shake.

Okay, this is it, she thought. *No way is he going to be as welcoming as his wife, or even the housekeeper, for that matter.*

To say she was surprised with the honest warmth reflected in his blue eyes—eyes that were identical to the man she'd once referred to as a blue-eyed devil—was putting it past mild.

"Honey, I told you about Ms. Adams joining us for dinner, right?" the woman asked, upping the wattage on her smile a hundredfold.

He smiled down at his wife. The arm he had casually wrapped around her waist when he'd first come by her side tightened just a fraction, the long fingers massaging the indenture of her waist.

Hmm. Interesting, Sinclair thought.

She caught the passing glance between the pair. It was…a conspirator's look they had exchanged.

Sinclair cataloged it. And promptly pushed it to the back of her mind for later contemplation.

"You mean the text you sent to the phone I left on our bedside table this morning? The phone that got trampled when I broke in one of the new horses? The phone

I asked, since you were headed to town, if you could take with you to see about getting me a new one? That phone?" He said with a mischievous glint in his eye.

His wife's feigned look of surprise didn't even look real to Sinclair, and she didn't know the woman.

Sonia bit her bottom lip, fighting the grin that Sinclair could see was tugging the corners of her generous mouth as she grinned unrepentantly up at her handsome husband.

She reached a hand up to pat his lean cheek. "Oh, baby, I forgot about that!" she replied. "I'm so sorry. Is there anything I can do to make up for it?" she asked, and again she had the butter-wouldn't-melt-in-her-mouth expression on her pretty face.

If anything, her grin deepened.

Against her will, Sinclair found herself intrigued by the couple's playing.

"Hmm. Maybe," he said, his gaze catching on her mouth before sliding up to her face. "I'm sure I can think of something. We'll talk about your punishment later tonight."

"Am I in trouble?" she asked. But the way she said it… Sinclair fought against a blush. She felt like a voyeur.

"You might be."

Sinclair caught the way Sonia's eyes widened and the look her husband gave her made Sinclair's blush break completely free.

She'd seen that same look on his brother's face just two days prior, when she'd been in his office.

Directed at her.

She felt a fine line of sweat bead on her brow and trickle down her cheek.

If she didn't know any better she'd swear she had bypassed her productive years and been slammed straight into menopause with the swamp of heat.

She felt her entire body heat up, wondering if it had been a good idea to accept the invitation to dinner, after all.

"I see you've met my brother and sister-in-law.... Please, don't mind them. Come on in."

All three turned when Nick's deep voice interrupted. Sinclair had never been so glad to hear his voice.

She, along with Sonia and Key, watched him walking down a long stretch of hallway, his strides eating up the distance before he was standing in the foyer with the trio.

"Don't mind us? What is *that* supposed to mean? You weren't even in the room, anyway," his brother scoffed. "How do you know there is a need for you to excuse our behavior?" Key asked, staring at Nick.

As the two men faced one another, Sinclair took the time to look at them both and was struck by their similarities.

But she was even more struck by the fact that although the two men were indeed identical twins, she knew that, without a doubt, she'd be able to tell them apart.

Both were tall, equally so. She knew that some twins, even identical twins, would sometimes have one that was either taller or heavier, or sometimes both.

Not in the case of these two rugged Hawaiian cowboys.

Both men wore scuffed-up cowboy boots with equally worn heels, so there was no height advantage for either twin.

She discreetly ran a glance over them.

Just as with their height, both had an impressive breadth of shoulders; wide shoulders that tapered down to a trim waist and thick, muscled thighs. Her gaze trailed to their faces.

Both were drop-dead gorgeous, with startling blue eyes and light golden-tanned skin. Their eyes were made even more vivid by the darkness of thick eyebrows and ridiculously long, sooty eyelashes.

Their aquiline noses were similar, right down to the small bump in the middle. She'd noted that both had that same bump and assumed it was from a sporting accident. It wasn't uncommon, she knew, for twins to fall into the same type of injuries.

Although both men wore their jet-black, shiny hair longer than tapered, Nick's was a few inches longer, the ends curling lightly and brushing the top of his collar.

Chiseled cheeks and a square chin completed a picture of rugged, uncommonly fine-looking men.

But for all that…she caught the difference: the small dimple near Nick's lower lip when he smiled. The way his lids would lower when he looked at her, as though he had something so naughty on his mind that he sought to hide it. He knew better than to let her see his eyes, knowing it would show.

Or the way, when he smiled, just one side of his

mouth would hitch upward and again, his hooded eyes would stare a hole into her, making her feel like some kind of prey caught in a fierce predator's focused sight...

He chose that moment to glance over at her and she felt the heat of that predator's stare. She was helpless to look away.

"I'm glad you could make it, Sinclair," he said. His voice seemed deeper, richer. A low, sexy rumble.

She grew warm and sweat pooled between her breasts.

"I gave Mahi a list of your demands... I mean, the foods you might like," he said, and she caught the twinkle in his eye and fought the urge to laugh along with him.

When he put out his hand for her to take, she hesitated before placing hers within his.

She turned and caught Sonia watching her, an odd expression on her face. When their eyes met, the other woman smiled at her and Sinclair felt oddly embarrassed.

The other woman had given her the type of look only a woman could give another that she knew was attracted...to a man.

The evening meal and accompanying conversation went quite smoothly. No great surprises, other than the fact that Sinclair was having one of the best times in the company of other adults that she'd had in longer than she wanted to think about.

Nick mentioned that he and Key ran the A'kela Ranch, while their father Alek Kealoha was recovering from a stroke.

She was glad to hear the patriarch was doing well in his recovery and would eventually start to take a more active role around his ranch.

At one point, as they began eating the homemade coconut ice cream Mahi had prepared for dessert, the topic went back to the documentary that Sonia had produced.

"I have no problem using my man for my business endeavors. In fact, he likes it, don't you, baby?" the other woman asked, and Sinclair's eyes widened at the obvious double entendre.

"Yes, baby. In fact, I'm going to let you know tonight just how much, dear," he said.

Sinclair saw the other woman's reddish brown face flush.

"I told you.... Freaks," Nick said drolly, a bored look on his face as he nodded his head toward his brother and sister-in-law. "You get used to it, though, Sinclair."

Although he'd made the comment, a light of humor blazed in his blue eyes and she'd seen the love he had not only for his brother, but obviously for his sister-in-law, as well.

They had all laughed at his feigned offense, including Sinclair.

A small smile played around her lips as she enjoyed the rest of the conversation, any tension she'd thought she'd encounter a distant thought.

Chapter 10

As the night moved on, Sinclair had been amazed at how the time had flown and how much of a good time she was having.

She had found that the brothers, both, had a wicked sense of humor. One that, had she not known any better, would make her think they were in fact blood relatives of the Wildes.

Yet the Wildes were not actually blood brothers, despite the similarity in their personalities. A lot of that had to do with them being raised together as brothers, under Clint Jedediah Wilde as their father.

Guilt assaulted her from two different camps. On the one side, she'd suddenly, eerily, gained an odd understanding of what the twins felt, knowing that Clint Wilde was their father yet never having known him. She could understand the anger and betrayal both men no doubt felt. Although Nick was open about his anger, his brother was silent. Yet Sinclair had found him looking at her throughout the meal, occasionally. In his blue eyes was not anger or mistrust…it was the exact opposite.

She'd felt confused, unsure of what was going on, why he seemed so much like family…

It was a disquieting thought, which in turn presented her with the other side.…

That one thought alone made her feel exceedingly guilty about her Wilde Boys. She was there for them… not to cozy up to the Kealohas, no matter how she may empathize with them.

After dinner and dessert, they took their coffee to one of the larger sitting rooms. Immediately, Sonia and Key sat, as though one, in a large chair that was meant for one but two could share. She smiled at the love between them. It was so palpable she felt as though, again, she was back home observing the Wildes with their spouses.

She felt Nick's eyes on her and her heart started thumping hard against her chest, a reaction she was starting to associate with him.

He reached out a hand for her to take, asking her, silently, to sit near him on the soft leather sofa. She took two steps before she halted and shook her head as though to clear it.

"Come and sit with me. I don't bite," he said and her face caught color as her eyes widened. She heard a choked-off laugh coming from Sonia but couldn't stop looking at him.

"Come on…you know you want to," he said and her blush deepened.

"Give the woman a break, Nick. She doesn't know you, yet," she heard his brother admonish from behind her, but still she was stuck, her gaze locked with his.

He smiled.

Her heart about stopped beating.

"Oh, yes, she does, brother," he murmured for her ears alone.

The blush intensified and she swallowed. She forced herself out of the odd trance he'd placed her under.

She straightened her back, lengthened her spine. Purposely she put on a sardonic look as she threw on her attitude like a well-worn coat.

"You're right.… I do," she said to Key before turning back to Nick. "Which is why I think I'll take this seat instead," she said, pointing a finger at the chair beside which she'd left her briefcase. Behind her she heard both Sonia and Key laugh outright.

Point: Sinclair.

Completely ignoring *his* knowing smile, Sinclair sat in the upright chair and brought her briefcase into her lap, strangely battling a smile she felt trying to break free.

She, with reluctance, pulled out the documents she'd brought with her.

"Listen…we trust you."

Before she could even withdraw all of the documents, Key had spoken.

Her eyes flew to meet Keanu's glance. "Excuse me?"

She could feel Nick's eyes on her and turned to see him sitting back on the leather sofa, a neutral look on his handsome face that didn't match the blazing look in his eyes.

"Of course we will look at the documents," Key continued, "but as I've told my brother, we are leaving this... decision for him to handle. We trust and believe in him." Key spoke calmly, as though not discussing what could be a volatile situation regarding millions of dollars at stake. "Whatever decision you two come up with is one that we, as a family, will agree to. Whatever that is," he finished.

His wife smiled down at him, kissed him. The moment was so private, a communication only the two of them understood, that Sinclair glanced away, her eyes colliding with Nick's.

"Looks like you're stuck with me, darlin'," he drawled, his hot glaze sliding over her body.

She fought the warmth flushing her body with his look.

"Hope that's all right with you?" he rasped, bringing the cup of coffee he held within his big, capable hands to his mouth.

"I think I can, uh, handle that," she said, putting the papers aside and toying with her own mug, her gaze locked with his.

"Good," he said, one side of his mouth lifting in that way he had, before he took a drink of the hot brew.

She watched in helpless fascination as he drank. The

way his throat worked the liquid down, the strong column of his neck straining as it slid down his throat.

She forgot for the moment that anyone was there but Nick. She even forgot why she'd come there.

There was *no one* in the room but the two of them.

"So, are you okay with that, Sinclair?"

Sinclair turned to see Sonia staring at her, a small smile lifting the corner of her generous mouth.

"I'm definitely good with that," she said, putting as much professionalism as possible into her voice and demeanor. "No problem for me."

The rest of the conversation proved pleasant, though before long Sinclair, surprised at the time, started to gather up her things. Standing, she said good-night to Key and Sonia and nodded when Nick offered to walk her to her car. It seemed natural for him to do so.

After walking her to her rental, he offered to shadow her back to her hotel.

"It's not a problem for me to do that. It's late, and although it's safe around here—the entire island is—I would feel better if you allowed me to see you back to your hotel safely."

She was already shaking her head no before he could finish.

"Um, no. I'm good. I mean, it's not that far of a drive. And, uh, like you said, the island is safe and—" She stopped as the dimple appeared near the lower corner of his mouth.

He was so sexy when he smiled like that. She nearly groaned out loud.

She knew she had to get away from him quick-fast and in a hurry. Throughout the evening they'd locked gazes and she'd known that he was too…experienced not to know she found him sexy as hell. And at this point, not only was it obvious that she felt attracted to him, but from the looks and his demeanor it was clear he was attracted to her, as well.

She was in a precarious position.

But she also knew his ego was just big enough that he would never think of forcing his attention on her. No, he was the type who enjoyed the woman chasing him.

She straightened her back, firmed her smile. Well, she wasn't that type of woman.

His eyes rolled over her face and stopped at her mouth.

With his gaze focused on her mouth, she licked lips gone completely dry, leaning away from him, fumbling in her satchel for her keys as her rear end bumped against the car door.

She glanced up in time to catch the knowing look in his vivid blue eyes at her telling response to his nearness.

"Well, thanks for a great evening. Your family is very nice. And I'll get back with you all on the new proposal. I mean *to* you, I guess, as it appears as though we're flying solo with this," she said in one long rushed sentence. She stopped and forced a smile she knew was twitchy from the nerves racking her. She turned, not wanting to make eye contact because she was too damn nervous to do so.

"Good night."

She would have gotten away with it, too, had he not stopped her, placed his big, warm hands on her shoulders and turned her back around to face him.

Goose bumps feathered down her arms when she felt his hands run down the length of her bared skin before holding her wrists.

She dropped her briefcase on the soft grass.

In a move that surprised her, he leaned down and captured her lips with his.

And just like that, she detonated.

His lips feathered back and forth over hers, casually, no demand, while his hands loosely bound her wrists.

When his tongue pressed against the seam of her lips she eagerly opened for him, eager for the feel of his tongue in her mouth. She'd imagined how it would feel, rough yet smooth.

She groaned when he lapped inside.

It was just as she'd imagined, but hotter. More intense.

He pulled her closer, one hand taking over as it kept her bound, the other moving to the back of her neck.

He was in control. Even as he kissed her, his lips making love to her mouth, a part of her recognized that he was a man used to being in control.

She allowed him the control, because it made her feel so damn good.

She moaned, leaning into the kiss and shyly meeting his tongue with hers.

He groaned harshly and brought her even tighter against his body, grinding against her so that she inhaled sharply against the sensation, feeling his shaft, thick, hard, against her stomach.

The kiss grew hotter and wetter as their tongues dueled.

A sound broke into her consciousness like an irritating buzz. She recognized it as the sound of men speaking, laughing, not far in the distance.

She brought her hands up to his chest and pushed him away.

Sinclair was so shaky she leaned against the car to lend her strength.

He reached out to grab her shoulders, and she moved away.

"I'm fine," she mumbled.

"I shouldn't have—"

"Look, it's fine. I'm a grown woman. I didn't let you do anything I didn't want done," she said, forestalling him from apologizing, her hand raised as she turned to lift her briefcase from the grass near the driveway where she'd allowed it to drop.

She glanced up at him in the dark, the moon highlighting his handsome face.

Instead of the look of triumph she expected to see, his was one of arousal mixed with something more…. That same thing she'd seen when they'd first met.

It was as though he was trying to peer into her soul.

Without a backward glance, she got into the car, reversed and skidded in her rush to leave before smoothly taking back control. Yet…she raced from the circular driveway as though the hounds of hell were after her.

With all of the heated stares and with all the sweating and panting she'd been doing the entire night, she felt just as though they were.

Chapter 11

She was a powder keg of sensuality, waiting to be lit.

He ran a hand across his face.

Nick couldn't take it anymore. The entire week he'd been on edge, his cock so hard he could use it to slice the Wagyu beef his family prided themselves on producing.

And the longer he watched her prance around his ranch, the randier he got. He didn't know how much longer he could take it before he would detonate.

And day by day it was getting worse.

It had been just a week, and he had it so bad for her, he was beginning to question his own sanity.

That morning he'd had a run-in with his brother. He'd known that his brother was aware that everything wasn't going exactly the way he'd planned with Sinclair the minute Key had opened his mouth.

* * *

"Everything cool, Nick?"

Without asking, he was asking.... It wouldn't take a rocket scientist to figure out that Key knew things weren't going that great.

Nick snorted. "That's got to be the understatement of the year."

He'd gotten up early this morning, earlier than the normal—5:00 a.m.—just to get out to the south pasture to look upon his land before it got busy and the ranch "came alive."

He often did that whenever something was heavy on his mind.

He glanced over at his brother. "How did *you* know?"

"That Sinclair is on your mind 24/7?"

Nick slowly nodded his head. There was no sense in trying to convince his brother that there wasn't something going on in his psyche regarding Sinclair.

His brother barked out a laugh.

"I remember the symptoms."

Nick didn't respond. He couldn't. He knew his brother was referring to how he had fallen for his wife. It wasn't like that for him. He wasn't falling in *love* with Sinclair...she just plagued his mind nonstop, he thought irritably.

At most, he was falling in lust with her.

The thought of how she'd feel beneath him had been his constant companion for the past week. In fact, it had been growing for six months, from their first communication.

"She's under my skin, man." Nick grumbled as the admission was torn from him. He knew that if he didn't just admit it, voice it, it would only get worse. Who better than his brother to admit it to? "Just not sure how in hell to get her out," he finished. He lifted the coffee mug to his mouth and took a swallow of the now-cooling brew.

"Who says she has to *come out,* so to speak?"

The two men stared out at the pasture, not looking at the other, both in their own thoughts.

Casually, as though it was no big deal, Key removed the large coffee mug from Nick's hand and took a deep swallow. Then promptly grimaced.

Before he could say a word and without even glancing his brother's way, Nick spoke into the silence. "You don't get to complain when you don't make it. That goes for when you steal it, as well."

Nick didn't *have* to look at his brother to know the look on his face after taking a drink of his coffee.

"Serves you right for taking such a big-ass gulp, anyway," Nick continued, snickering.

His lack of coffee-making skills was one of many reasons why Mahi forbade him from being in the kitchen when he was preparing any given meal.

"It's something about her..." Nick began, only to stop, shake his head. He paused for a long moment before continuing. "Something about how damn protective she is of her 'Wilde Boys.'" Nick picked the topic back up, unaware that one side of his lip had curled slightly downward when he mentioned the Wildes.

"Nick...brother, look," Key began with a sigh. He

took a careful drink of the coffee before he placed a
booted foot on the lower log of the fence and propped his
large elbows on the top rail. Although he'd complained,
Nick noticed he didn't give him back his coffee.

"There are a few things you need to figure out, and
one of them most definitely isn't how to 'get' Sinclair
out of your head. One of them is how you feel about the
Wildes," Key stated.

"Aw, hell, I don't need to hear——"

"And all this crap about being 'over' the fact that Clint
either didn't know about us, or care enough to find out,
is the major bee in your bonnet," Key said, talking over
his brother's protest.

"It's not that, Key. I couldn't give a damn… Wait.
'Bee in my bonnet'? Really, bro, that's the best you have?
You've been hanging around your wife too long. You're
getting soft," he said, unable to let that one go.

When his brother gave him the middle-finger salute to his observation, he continued. "Look, if the man
knew, cared, or otherwise, I don't care. That's all in the
past." He stopped, his brow knitting in a frown. "A past
I have…or had…no intention of dredging up. I'd decided
to let it all go, anyway, to move on. Before…"

His brother turned to face him, an equal frown on his
face. "Okay…this is new. 'Before'? Before what? What
are you talking about?"

Nick ran a frustrated hand through his hair, feeling
conflicting emotions as his brother stared at him, his
eyes boring a hole through Nick.

"Damn. Look… Before Sinclair came around, before

she informed me she wanted to come out to the ranch to settle this, I was ready to let it drop."

"And?" Key prompted when it looked as though Nick wasn't going to continue.

He shrugged his wide shoulders. "And I didn't."

"No damn way. You can't just say that and not explain. You need to, if for no other reason than it's going to help *you* understand. Don't you see that?" The look in his brother's eyes was disconcerting. As though his brother knew something he didn't, as though he understood something Nick didn't.

Nick growled in frustration.

"It wasn't Wilde's...fault. He didn't know about us. Mom never told him. I know that. I just—" He stopped, clenched his teeth.

Although Key had asked the question, it was less than a minute later when Nick realized his brother had realized, come up with, surprised or Jedi-mind-tricked him. Either way his brother laughed.

Shaking his head, Nick turned back to face the south pasture. The sun was beginning to rise, and the two men observed it together. The ranch was beginning to come alive.

The brothers didn't exchange another word about the topic. Key instinctively realized his brother needed to get a handle on his feelings for not only Clint Wilde, but more importantly for the woman who was intimately involved with the family of a man he hated.

He glanced over at his brother, his twin. A small

smile pulled the corners of his mouth. He clapped his brother on the back.

"Yeah, well, I'm sure you can handle one little lady, brother, can't you?" he laughed, reminding Nick of how he'd once teased Key about Sonia. "Funny how karma and life find a way of getting us all eventually, huh?" Again his brother laughed. He laughed so hard he nearly choked.

Nick didn't think it was so damn funny.

Chapter 12

Sinclair stood at the gate closure, watching as Nick slowly approached the stallion. The animal tossed its head back, its nostrils flaring in agitation and its eyes on Nick, carefully watching as he approached.

The stallion was one of the most magnificent horses Sinclair had ever seen, which was saying a lot as she'd grown up on a ranch known for its acquisition of quality horses.

She frowned as she stared at the golden horse, trying to recall the name of the particular breed. She was no expert, but as she'd grown up around horses, she was very familiar with many types. It was magnificent: golden in color, nearly platinum, with a metallic-like bloom to its coat. The sun's rays bounced and played off the animal's body, enhancing the effect.

Yet, even with the natural majesty of the beautiful animal, it was Nick and Nick alone who held Sinclair's attention.

The man had more swagger than any man she'd ever met. Natural swagger, something that was innate to a man and couldn't be taught, learned or imitated; either he had it or he didn't. And Nick had *it*.

His natural charm was intoxicating.

She kept her eyes trained on the action ahead, blocking out everything else even as the noise from around her grew louder.

She'd known from the chatter around the ranch that he'd bought a new horse. A gorgeous and rare stallion, but one that was near wild from what she'd heard in the cowboys' excited comments.

When she'd heard Nick was about to "break" it, she'd carefully gathered the documents that she had been working on in the office and put them away. The fact that the documents weren't ones pertaining to the Wildes and the Kealohas, but related to another case she was working on made her feel uncomfortable.

She and Nick hadn't gone over the latest offer she'd put together. Each time she brought the topic up, he found something to distract her, from taking her to one of the orchards or gardens that his mother's foundation supported, to showing her around the small community, to taking her to hideaway cafés that the tourists weren't aware of.

All along she was getting to know him, discovering

that beyond the fine exterior, the player image she'd so easily bought into, was so much more.

It was that "more" that had her worried. But she kept her perspective, and although she'd contacted the Wildes, she was told, just as Nick had been told by his brother, that she was "in charge."

There were times, in the back of her mind, that she thought about it and wondered at both sides putting the situation solely into their hands. As well, she felt guilty for working on things for her few other clients, work that had nothing to do with the reason she was in Hawaii, but she forced the nagging feelings away.

"I think I'm going to head out and check out what's going on," she had said earlier as she'd stood from the leather chair and pushed away from the small desk.

She'd smiled at Ailani who had offered earlier in the week to share "office" space if she needed it, surprising Sinclair with her generosity.

"I heard the men bought a new mare. An Akhal-Teke," she'd said, frowning, hoping she'd pronounced it correctly. "I've never seen that breed in real life." She'd said that, knowing that it was best to at least tell a partial truth than a complete lie.

If Ailani decided to come out and saw Sinclair watching the excitement, maybe she wouldn't know that it was Nick who'd attracted her and not the animal. At least, that was her hope.

Ailani had glanced up from her own computer and smiled distractedly. "Oh, yeah, sure. It's a gorgeous animal! Nick and I bought it from auction a couple of weeks ago," she'd said, smiling. Sinclair had nodded, returning the smile. She'd felt just the smallest nod of jealousy but put it away. After the time she'd been at the ranch, she realized that Nick and Ailani were no more than friends. In fact their relationship was close, and very similar to what Sinclair had with the Wildes.

She'd been spending more and more time with Nick this past week, getting to know him, learning his likes and dislikes as he was learning hers.

She felt that queasy-good sensation in the pit of her stomach that a woman felt when she knew a man was as into her as she was into him. She'd hurried along to check him out, in action.

She stood along with the others near the enclosure, a gated-off area that she'd learned they used for the wilder horses they often bought at auction. Horses that many of the surrounding ranchers who attended the private auction thought were too much bother to buy. No matter how good the bloodline, no one was willing to potentially lose a great deal of money on a horse they couldn't break.

Her eyes left the beautiful animal and stayed on Nick. He was all alpha male, from the top of his dark head to the bottom of his big cowboy-boot-wearing feet.

Besides her own growing feelings, Sinclair saw what the appeal was for him, his brother and the entire Kealoha ranch for that matter, and what made their reality show the mega hit that it was.

Raw, masculine heat.

Her glance slid around the ranch. There were always

female tourists around, no matter what. Although they weren't supposed to be within certain staff-only areas, some wheedled the younger cowboys into giving them access and the young men had eagerly brought them, only to be embarrassed when Ailani read them the riot act for doing so.

Currently they were not filming the show, for which Sinclair was grateful. Yet there seemed to be an inordinate number of women on the ranch, hanging around the Visitors Only section. Although they allowed visitors on the ranch, most of the ranch was off limits to those who didn't live on, or work at, the Kealoha ranch.

She knew that the Kealohas had more recently had begun to allow a small number of tourists to come to the ranch, outside of the visitors for the show, to a designated section. They'd even decided to give a few "dude" lessons, all for donations to the Aloha Keiki foundation they'd started in honor of their mother.

For all the sheer masculinity and testosterone teeming around the ranch, there was also heart. Although the locale and people were different, there was a similar, *familiar* vibe at the Kealoha ranch, one that reminded her of the Wyoming Wilde Ranch.

Most of the hands had been at this ranch for years, like Ailani Mowry, the ranch's foreman. Sinclair had not been sure what to expect from Ailani initially, but she had to admit she was all business when it came to the ranch. And the men she managed seemed to respect her, as well, from what Sinclair had determined so far, in the limited time she'd been at the ranch.

Sinclair still wasn't sure how she felt about the woman on a personal level; she'd wait and hold judgment. Although she had a feeling that behind the woman's reserved demeanor, the one she showed to Sinclair, was a more vivacious personality. One she chose only to show to those she knew and or cared about. Like Key and Nick.

Nick.

She sighed.

Piggybacking that thought was the realization that her thoughts and actions, from the moment she woke up excited to head out to see the Kealoha ranch…and Nick… had been so caught up in him, that she'd not missed home.

She experienced a pang when she thought of the Wilde Ranch. She'd expected…*wanted*…to miss it more than she did.

The truth was that since her arrival and during all the time they'd spent together, she hadn't. She put those disconcerting thoughts away, both about the Wilde Ranch and her confusing feelings toward Nick.

Just to watch Nick break in a horse.

Yeah…that makes a heck of a lot of sense, her inner voice mocked. She sighed again and leaned into the fence, her eyes glued on Nick as he slowly approached the stallion.

"He doesn't even use a blind."

Startled, Sinclair turned, surprised to see Ailani standing near her. She'd been so wrapped up in her own thoughts she hadn't realized the other woman was in the area.

"So I see," Sinclair replied, familiar with the term the foreman had used.

Having grown up on the Wilde Ranch, she was as comfortable with cowboy lingo as she was with legal briefs. "Is he an adept bronc buster?" she asked, thinking of Nate Wilde, who was an expert at breaking in the more unruly horses the ranch acquired.

The foreman tilted her head to the side, a small smile creasing her full lips

"Very impressive. Oh, that's right, you grew up on a ranch. I'd forgotten that."

Sinclair scrutinized her face, her voice, looking for any hint of sarcasm, but found none. Her expression was open, honest. Sinclair relaxed and turned back to the scene in front of her.

"Yes. Though all the men at the Wilde Ranch are adept at breaking horses, Nate is the best at it, to be honest. It was how he helped make money for the ranch when he and his brothers were young men," she replied, hearing the pride in her own voice and not caring if the woman heard it.

"Well, I guess the…brothers have that in common, as well?"

Sinclair gave the woman a glance, again wondering at her motive.

"Nate is the expert, but his other two brothers, Shilah and Holt, are no strangers to breaking in a horse. They've all worked hard to see the ranch a success." Purposely,

Sinclair included the three Wildes, although she knew the woman was linking Nick as a Wilde, alluding to the fact that he was the son of Clint Jedediah Wilde.

"They're like family to you, the Wildes, aren't they?" Ailani asked after a slightly awkward pause.

"Look, I'm not sure what is going on here. I don't know your connection with Nick, or how involved you are in this matter between the Wildes and the Kealohas, but for the record I am here in the best interest of the Wildes and their holdings. And that is it," she said, feeling on the defensive even as she was embarrassed, knowing good and well the foreman hadn't made the comment with the intent of being nasty.

"For the record, Ms. Adams... I have no pony in that race, as the saying goes," Ailani said.

Had it not been for the slightly reddish tinge to her café-au-lait skin, Sinclair wouldn't have known she'd upset the woman. She felt immediately chagrined at her own behavior and just a little bit ridiculous.

She'd been less than her normal cordial self with the foreman and she knew the reason for that was not because the woman had said or done anything besides be close to Nick.

Sinclair was woman enough to admit when she was wrong. "I'm sorry. I have a lot on my mind lately and... well..." She shook her head. "I didn't mean anything."

Ailani shrugged her narrow shoulders. "Hey...no problem. I get like that with my 'boys,' too," she said, laughing softly as she gazed over at Nick.

Sinclair refused to allow the kernel of jealousy to rear

its ugly head again. Enough was enough. Besides, she had no claim on Nick Kealoha.

He was just a job.

She paid no heed to the uproarious mocking laughter in her head that came with the thought.

Hush, she quieted the voice.

"I don't know anything about the Wildes except what's common knowledge. Just like my boys…the Wildes are just an internet search away. Information just a keystroke away. And as I'm sure you know, not everything you read is true," Ailani replied, her voice lowering, her gaze unflinching as she looked at Sinclair.

Sinclair kept her gaze just as steady on the foreman, reading the underlying message she was delivering easily. Then the other woman surprised her, her gaze softening.

"Your Wildes…they seem like good men. Just as the Kealohas are. And just as you are protective of them, I feel the same sense of loyalty for the Kealohas," she said. She pushed away from the fence post after glancing over at the scene in front of her, of Nick and the animal, surrounded by ranch hands as they cheered him on.

She surprised Sinclair when she finished with, "And just like you and the Wildes, they are the only living family that I have."

The two women held glances for long moments, neither one moving away, neither one dropping the other's gaze.

How the foreman knew that she was alone in the world, except for the Wildes, Sinclair had no clue.

She mentally shrugged. But, as the woman said…the internet was just a keystroke away.

Sinclair was adept at reading people. What she was now reading from the woman was…love. Love for the Kealohas' A'kela Ranch. The same love she herself had for the Wilde Ranch.

If for no other reason, this made her relax.

"I have a good feeling about you. I'm sure all of this will be resolved in a fair manner and…swiftly, Ms. Adams. Good day, ma'am," Ailani said. And with that, she jammed the beat-up, wide-brimmed, faded-pink cowboy hat onto her head, pulled the long braid from beneath and allowed it to flop in front of her shoulder—a style Sinclair had seen the woman wear each time she'd spied her on the ranch.

She stared after the woman, a contemplative look on her face.

Had she just been warned off and welcomed both at the same time? she wondered.

Sinclair felt an unreasonable smile threaten to break free. The longer she was on the ranch, the more she was strangely feeling like she was…home. The people reminded her so much of those at the Wilde Ranch.

"You got him, boss! You did it!"

Sinclair's attention was diverted from the woman and back to what was going on inside the small corral

In the short time she'd been in conversation with Ailani, Nick had been successful in breaking the horse. While she knew that it would take another session before the horse was ready to interact with the others, as well as be used by the other cowboys, she was impressed.

He was good. Damn good.

Her gaze ran over him. He was more than good…

His Levi's were dirty and had seen more wear than any pair of jeans should. Although he wore a belt, complete with a buckle that bore the Kealoha crest—she knew, as she'd noticed it when he'd worn it before—they rode low on his hips, his shirt bearing evidence of a long day's work.

Helpless to look away, Sinclair watched as he laughed at something one of the other men said to him, his strong white teeth gleaming in the sunlight. It was then he turned and their glances caught.

She noticed, peripherally, the same cowboy glance her way and then say something to Nick.

She couldn't hear what he said from the distance, although she had fairly good lip-reading abilities— abilities she'd acquired in law school during court sessions—and instinctively knew she was the topic of conversation.

She *should* be angry.

Or at the very least curious as to why the man was obviously talking about her…or what he was saying. When she saw another man join them, and all three glanced at her, she should've at least been uncomfortable.

Should've been.

But as she stared at Nick and their gazes held, she didn't really care what the others had said or were saying.

Nick and Nick alone captured and held her attention.

She watched as he blindly handed the horse's bridle and bit to one of the waiting men. After dusting his hands down the sides of his filthy jeans, he jammed his cowboy hat onto his dark head and ambled toward her.

She swallowed, taking in the sexy sight of him as his long legs devoured the distance. The man was the walking definition of sexy.

She felt moisture in her panties, a reaction she was now growing accustomed to having whenever she was around Nick Kealoha.

She should leave. She should go back to the assigned office space she'd been given to work out of if necessary and just...leave.

She couldn't. Instead she remained rooted to the spot.

And waited for him to come to her.

It had been a week of them dancing around each other.

She swallowed the excitement...and fear, biting her lower lip, tugging it deeply into her mouth, unaware of the picture she presented.

Chapter 13

Although the ranch was teeming with activity and men were gathered around watching as Nick began the task of breaking the stallion, Nick was acutely aware of Sinclair watching him.

His glance ran over the stallion as *it* watched him, warily. He needed to keep his head in the game, Nick knew. Breaking a damn-near-wild horse was no playing matter.

The horse threw its head back and snorted, before lowering its head. Its nostrils flared as it exhaled a deep breath.

Nick had known it the minute Sinclair had come within…smelling distance. He'd felt much like the animal in front of him. His sense of smell, as well as everything else, became acute, animalistic, when it came to Sinclair Adams.

They'd been sniffing around each other for the past week. It was all he could do not to take her to one of the stalls and have his way with her. But he'd played it cool. Let his guard down enough to let her in, to show her who he really was.

He knew what her thoughts were about him: playboy and wealthy cowboy. It was an image he'd carefully cultivated. But he'd found that with her, he wanted her to get to know him, not the image.

Damn. It wasn't the smartest move on his part: letting the enemy close.

But she'd never been the enemy. She'd been anything but an enemy. From the first moment they'd spoken, the first email, she'd sparked his interest.

He ran a gaze over her as he approached her.

Today she wore a pretty peach sleeveless dress, the color a perfect foil to her golden-brown skin, her arms and shoulders exposed, the skin looking so soft. He couldn't wait to get his hands on it.

He'd found every damn excuse in the book to touch her over the past week, casual touches, when she would come to his office or when he helped her walk over the plants in the orchard.

He knew that he needed more than just casual touches. He needed her beneath him as he rocked into her softness, felt her warmth surround him as he stared into her eyes while they made love.

He bit back a curse.

She made his cock rock-hard within seconds, while making him think.

Think about what it was he was angry about. Who? Why?

He frowned, pushing back the memories, the thoughts. Right now, as whenever he was around her, he found he didn't want to think of anything or anyone else that might interfere with them.

He knew he had it bad for her and didn't give a damn. Not now.

Although the corral was teeming with cowboys, it could have been a ghost town as far as he was concerned.

For that moment it was only the two of them.

And he knew that he had to do something about the way he felt about her. It had been only a week that she'd been at the ranch, but that, with the six months they'd been communicating, which felt like six months of foreplay, made him a powder keg ready to blow.

When he stepped outside the enclosure and approached her, he stopped, an unknowing smile on his face.

His gaze raked over her face, down the long line of her slender neck, to the deep V of her dress, where her small, perfectly round breasts crested over the top of her bra.

He saw her nipples pucker beneath the dress and growled low in his throat, dragging his eyes away to meet hers.

He loved that he could make her body react like that.

His shaft hardened uncomfortably in his jeans.

He reached out and brought her hand to his mouth. He knew some of his men were watching. Didn't really give a damn.

He'd had enough. He was about to claim what was his. Even if she was his for a short time, until it was her time to go, or when this fever that had claimed him relented. For now, she was his.

He was about to claim what was his. Tonight.

"Have dinner with me tonight?" he asked, his voice low, rough with need.

He saw her eyes widen and her pulse bang against the soft line of her throat.

He felt a need to conquer her. To take her and have his way with her.

He moved nearer, truly unaware of what he was doing, his actions one of a man going blindly on instinct. Like a wild animal.

He brought a hand up to her waist, bringing her close to him. To that part of him he wanted to wreak havoc with, claim and dominate her with, like a stallion claiming his mare.

In the background, as though from a distance, he heard the snorting of the animal he'd just broken as it allowed his men to take it away.

He kept his focus on Sinclair.

"You'll be coming home with me afterward." The promise was low, so low his voice was barely above a gravelly rumble within his chest.

He saw that little pulse of hers jackhammer against the soft skin of her throat before he ran a tongue over it, then lightly bit her, claiming her.

Chapter 14

When Nick asked Sinclair to go out again, this time with them alone, she could tell that her agreement surprised him.

Not to mention the hot words he'd whispered—no, promised—against her neck. She shivered at the memory. It was more like a heated sexual threat, one that shouldn't have turned her on as much as it had, as it still did. But, God, it did.

After he'd made his decree she'd known that he'd realized, too late, how it sounded.

So demanding.

Claiming her.

And even more, Sinclair had known her agreement surprised him, particularly after she'd followed it up with a kiss, which she leaned on tiptoe to plant on his cheek. Along with a whispered agreement against his ear.

She'd bit the lower flesh of his ear and he'd stared down at her, the expression on his face one she'd never forget.

Making her feel her *power* as a woman.

Yes, there was no denying he was a dominant, sexual, alpha man. One she just might allow to…lead her, she thought, a purely feminine smile on her face as she glanced at him over her shoulder and slowly ambled away.

Knowing his gaze was straight on her butt, she'd put a little extra something-something in her sway.

Two could play at that game.

If nothing else, the fact that she had been able to surprise him, turn the tables on him, show him that it was she who gave him the power and that he wasn't taking it from her…made her feel good. Damn good.

She grinned as she applied her lipstick. For a nanosecond, at least, she'd had the upper hand.

Her time at the Kealoha ranch had been one of lots of twists and turns. From their first meeting to now, she hadn't known what to expect from Nick Kealoha. And she knew that was exactly what he'd wanted: to keep her off kilter.

She stared into the mirror, a contemplative look on her face.

"It might be fun," she said to her reflection. "A date… with Nick Kealoha." She stopped, shaking her head and laughing lightly, softly. That just sounded so tame, but she knew it wasn't going to be. He had already told her. And although she'd flirted with the notion of going back to his home with him, to make love, as she knew that was what he meant—no grown man said he was going to take you home to play board games, after all—would she really go through with it?

Is that what this was? A date?

The first time she'd had dinner with him had really just been a meeting between her and his family, a time where she'd gotten to see with whom she was dealing.

She'd expected the worst. She'd thought that, like Nick, the rest of the family was as anti-Wilde as he was.

She'd been surprised to find out just how wrong she'd been and since then, the family had been just as welcoming to her as they had been during that first meeting. She'd even met the elder Kealoha earlier in the week. He, like his sons and daughter-in-law, had been pleasant.

She snorted...not that she was expecting "pleasant" with Nick.

Pleasant wasn't exactly the way she would call her interactions with Nick. That was entirely too mild a word to describe the way he made her feel.

Confusing, funny, perplexing, infuriating...hot. He brought a bevy of emotions and feelings to the surface. But pleasantness was *not* one of them.

"A date. Just the two of us?" she asked her image aloud.

"Girl, no. Get yourself together. This is just a business conversation and nothing more. The quicker we can come to an agreement, the better. What's the worst that can happen?"

Peering into the mirror closer, she examined her face, scrunched her nose, frowning... Was she looking for traces of self-denial, maybe?

She lifted a shoulder and made a self-mocking moue at her own reflection.

Maybe.

Or maybe it was the irritating little pimple that was trying its best to form on her chin. Just what she needed, dang it.

Carefully, she applied her favorite Mac cream-to-powder foundation over the red mark before lightly dusting her face.

Usually she wore a minimum of makeup: a light dusting of translucent powder, and mascara to darken her lashes and light-colored or sheer lip gloss. The lip gloss protected against both the harsh winters and hot summers back in Wyoming.

But this time she wanted—needed—the full "armor."

She wanted everything in her arsenal. She had an idea what the night had in store for her, and she wanted to look her best.

With the determination of a general preparing for battle, she unzipped the small makeup bag packed with all her favorites.

As she deftly, expertly, began to apply her makeup, she tried to remain calm about the night in front of her.

She frowned absently at her image in the mirror, turning her head to each side to make sure she'd applied the makeup subtly.

Sinclair wanted to look good. Not like a made-up clown headed to a rodeo.

She laughed at herself, thinking of one of the many colorful sayings Miss Lilly kept in her arsenal. "Locked and loaded...and ready to unleash."

A small smile played around her full lips as she thought of Miss Lilly...or Mama Lilly, as most of the kids who, like Sinclair, had grown up with Lilly as a mother figure, called her.

Before she'd left for Hawaii, she'd spoken with the older woman, gleaning wisdom from her, as usual. But she'd left...sad. It was as though she was saying goodbye to the woman she'd long felt was a mother to her. Which made no sense. She'd felt the same way after Nate had said his final words to her, before she'd left the ranch for the airport the following day. Her grief indeed made no sense.

As soon as her business was conducted and done... she was headed back home.

Yet, even as she thought about it, Sinclair knew that some major decisions were in front of her.

She'd come to realize that as much as she loved the Wildes—they were, after all, like family—as well as the ranch life—the only life she'd known for all of her twenty-seven years—she was ready for a change. Though she wasn't sure what that change was or what form it would take.

She sighed deeply, shoving those thoughts to the back of her mind.

One hurdle at a time, she reminded herself.

She felt that queasiness enter her belly again, the kind you felt when your belly bottomed out on a roller coaster. It was the same feeling she got when she thought of Nick and his hot sexual threat.

She slowly rolled her head from side to side and fought for composure, determined to hold on for the ride.

Chapter 15

"If you're on the menu, I'm going for takeout. Damn."

Sinclair's eyes widened at the very cheesy line that came out of Nick's mouth the minute she walked up to him, meeting him in the hotel lobby.

Her startled gaze met his and when she saw the humor lurking in his deep blue eyes, she laughed, relaxing.

"What? You don't like that one?"

She shook her head no, laughing.

"Damn. And I spent the entire day working on it!" he said and she laughed outright again.

"Well, keep on trying," she said, laughing again, immediately relaxing against him as he escorted her out of the hotel and into the warm breezy night.

She glanced up at him, smiling, and her smile slipped just a little.

He was such a beautiful man. Beyond handsome. The man was gorgeous.

He tilted his head to the side, silently asking what was wrong as he glanced down at her, his hand lightly cupping her elbow as they stood outside waiting for his vehicle to be brought to them by the valet. She shook her head, a smile on her face.

"Beautiful night," she said, glancing around.

She'd been to Hawaii once before in undergraduate school, and had even done a tour of the major islands, but she didn't recall it being so beautiful, the air so warm yet crisp.

"Yes, it is," he said.

She glanced up at him and felt her confidence slip at the discerning look in his eyes.

He brought a thumb up to touch her face, his finger caressing her chin.

He wasn't talking about the night.

He brought their lips together in a brief kiss, too brief, before releasing it when the valet smoothly delivered his vehicle curbside. After tipping the uniformed man, he escorted her to her door, then jogged to the driver's side.

"I have the perfect place to take you. You're going to love what's on the menu," he promised.

This time there was no double entendre, nothing at all that should have had her holding back a groan. Fear and anticipation warred for dominance as he smiled over at her, his white teeth gleaming in the dark cab of his truck.

Dear God. She was in trouble. Deep, deep…deep trouble, she thought, smiling back at him weakly.

* * *

Surprisingly, dinner had been amazingly…uncomplicated, for Sinclair.

Yes, the sexual tension was there. Wasn't any way it wouldn't be with the way they'd been dancing around each other.

She wasn't going to even try to pretend that she didn't find him sexually exciting…she was sure there wasn't a woman alive who could claim that. In fact, their banter had increasingly become hotter and more exciting. What they'd begun six months ago was finally being realized. She suspected even he hadn't been aware, to the extent they now were, of exactly what they'd been doing since their first communication.

But Nick had done something very subtle, yet she'd caught it. Initially his sexual energy had been raw, palpable…and nearly overwhelming. She remembered the feeling of being run over by a Mack truck. The feeling hit her and kept on hitting. Battering, unrelenting.

The feeling of being prey for the big lion she'd imagined him to be earlier.

But somehow, as the time they'd spent together had increased, and they'd been around each other more, something else had changed, as well.

Yes, he was still devastatingly sexy and overwhelmingly…male. And yes, he still made her panties wet with one heated look.

But he was more…approachable. Approachable as in the fear of being swallowed whole by him had slightly diminished, she thought.

She shook her head, an unknown smile on her face.

She took another small spoonful of the creamy custard the waiter had delivered right as Nick had left to take a call. She'd promised to wait for him before she tried the dessert if it came.

She'd lied.

"Hmm," she murmured. She'd never had coconut custard of this variety before. "Too good," she said aloud and ran the spoon back and forth over the dessert to smooth it out so he couldn't tell she'd tried it. She glanced over her shoulder to see if he was coming.

"Should I be jealous of the custard?" The deep voice that broke into the love affair she had going on with the custard, startled Sinclair, making her cough a little. She was thankful she'd managed to swallow before that happened, as the last thing she wanted was for him to see her spewing custard from her nose.

Not sexy.

"Started without me, huh? Can't say that I blame you."

She watched as he took his chair, a chagrined smile on her face. "Sorry. Couldn't resist," she said around a mouthful of the delicacy. She frowned. "For such a big guy, you sure can tiptoe up on a woman," she grumbled, and he laughed outright. She responded to his laugh with a grin.

Even his bark of a laugh made her squirm, she thought, watching as he began to dig into his own dessert.

God, is there anything he doesn't do sexy?

"Hmm... I don't know. My brother has lied for years that I snored as a kid. I didn't. He did." He spoke around the spoonful of custard, the smile on his face causing a fizzle in the area of her stomach.

It took a minute for his comment to register.

When it did, her face heated up. She ducked her head, so embarrassed she wanted to crawl under the table. And low-crawl all the way out of the restaurant.

"Did I say that out loud?" she was almost afraid to ask.

"Yeah," he said and winked at her. "I'm too sexy for this custard." The wink was so exaggerated along with the silly quip that again he had her giggling and at ease. If she wasn't careful she could really fall for him, she thought.

As she watched him eat, that half smile of his in place as he kept her gaze, she wondered if it was too late. The spoon dangled in her hand.

He frowned. "Don't get all delicate on me now," he said. "Eat your dessert!"

"Actually, I'm full. As good as this is, I'm going to have to have it wrapped up," she replied, forcing a smile.

He raised a brow. "So you're telling me the woman that managed to put away that feast we ate...can't take on a small helping of coconut-custard ice cream and whipped cream? No way! I'm not buying it," he replied as he picked up his own spoon.

The laugh that bubbled up was unexpected. There was something about him that at times made her squirm and at other times made her want to laugh.

Although she knew she needed to be careful around Nick, she couldn't help the way her guard seemed to naturally relax around him.

"So what are you trying to say? If I recall correctly, I wasn't the only one, um…enjoying the meal," she said tongue-in-cheek and laughed when he nodded his head in agreement.

"No, but in my defense, I am six feet five inches and weigh two twenty-five. But you…" He stopped and stared at her, his gaze running over her as though he was examining her. "What are you… like five-five and ninety pounds, wringing wet?" he said, his eyes assessing her.

Two things happened. She was only a few inches over five feet, so his giving her extra inches gave him points. And guessing her weight at only ninety pounds…well, she wanted to kiss him for saying that alone.

She knew he was being funny, lighthearted, but the way his gaze went over her, especially the "wringing wet" part…it was as though his hands were touching, feeling her.

Keep it light, girl, keep it light, she reminded herself. And purposely took a *big* spoonful of the custard and winked at him as she did so.

"I was hungry," she said, shrugging. "I may be small, but I can eat," she said and he laughed along with her. "And never let it be said that Sinclair Cross Adams allowed a little custard to get the best of her!"

With that, and with relish, she polished off the remainder of her dessert, keeping the silly giggle from erupting from her mouth at the faux look of amazement that crossed his handsome face as he watched her take the last bite.

And lick the spoon. Front and back.

"Delicious. Down to the last…bite," he said. Just like that, he affected her.

She decided that the idea of air-conditioned undies was something she was seriously considering inventing herself.

Chapter 16

"Well… Thank you for the evening. It was…nice," Sinclair said, the inane words that tumbled from her lips the best she could come up with.

She glanced away and searched for the keycard in her purse, pretending to have a hard time finding it, if only to give her that much more time to get it together.

When his big hand reached inside her bag and pulled out the small keycard, handing it to her, she smiled up at him.

The look in his blue eyes made her inhale a deep steadying breath of much needed air.

And to think she had thought him…tame…if even for a moment, she thought, her heart racing.

"Dinner was delicious, thank you," she continued, staring at his mouth as they sat inside his vehicle. She wondered how she would survive the ride back to her hotel, thinking of the hot sensual promise he'd delivered, wondering if he'd been simply trying to get a reaction out of her.

She could not stop staring at the lower swell of what had to be the most sensual mouth she'd ever seen on a man. Could a man's mouth be more perfect?

The thought ran in her mind and Sinclair licked her lips, which had gone dry.

He turned toward her, one finger poised over the button that would turn on the ignition. He paused in the act, tipped his head forward. His hand reached out and lightly grasped the back of her head, bringing her closer.

The kiss was light, smooth…and devastating. When he released her, she slumped.

"You're amazing…has anyone ever told you that? I wonder if your Wilde Boys know how lucky they are," he mumbled, his eyes trained on her lips—making her heart race even harder—as though he wanted to kiss her again. Although they'd just eaten, he had the look of a man ready to feast.

What do I say to that? Sinclair wondered, breaking contact with his eyes and licking her lips again.

She ducked her head, staring down at her feet, as though the answer could be found in the open-toe heels.

Still, he didn't start the engine. He simply sat there staring at her. They were parked in one of the more isolated parts of the restaurant's rear lot. As it hadn't been a tourist hot spot, the restaurant hadn't been overly crowded, so his truck was the only one of a few parked in the back lot.

He reached over and tilted her chin up, forcing her to look back into his eyes.

"This is not for any reason except that I've been staring at your mouth the whole evening... No, since the moment I first laid eyes on your picture and wondered if they were half as soft as they looked," he murmured.

Her heart nearly leaped out of her chest.

"But...we've kissed. You already know what they feel like," she whispered in reply, half teasing.

That lone dimple appeared near his lower lip when he smiled. "Yeah, but I need to kiss you again, just to make sure the first few times weren't a fluke," he replied, his voice low, sexy and deep.

When his head descended, she reached up and met him in the kiss, her arms circling his neck to pull him near.

That was all the encouragement he needed.

He surprised her when he lifted her from her seat and over to him, straddling her legs across his. The roominess of his luxury truck made it an effortless venture and her eyes widened.

"Nick!"

"I love it when you call my name," he said and laughed, claiming her mouth immediately.

In the position he had her, she was unable to move.

Her hands flattened on his broad, hard chest, as his mouth worked magic over hers, grinding their lips together even as he ground his hardening shaft against her.

Kissing and moaning noises filled the cab as they took their fill of each other, kissing with a ferocity that mimicked what their bodies craved from one another.

The moment was beyond magical. The entire evening had been like something out of a dream.

Static, erotic energy arced back and forth between them, shooting from his hard body to hers, igniting electric blazes in its path.

The hand on the back of her head reached up to loosen the pretty chignon she'd placed it in earlier. Within moments her hair fell and his hand was buried inside it, massaging her scalp as he claimed her mouth.

She grew warm, her body opening to his as his hands reached around her, both on the small of her waist… and moved her.

She moaned against the feel of him. Excited beyond measure at the thought of what deliciousness lay hidden behind the dark dress pants he wore. How it would look exposed…. That part of him that, as he kissed and caressed her, ground against her, hardened to granite against her, intimately pressing into her stomach.

His length excited her, as she imagined what it would look like unleashed.

How it would feel inside her.

He excited her in ways she'd not felt in a long time. In ways she'd never felt.

When his hand reached out and lightly pulled her dress up, it felt…good.

When he pressed her even tighter against his body,

his hand on her ass, her hands clenched his shirt and she moaned into his mouth.

Trapped, powerless…she was on fire. He released her and she cried out. In the dark she saw his nostrils flare as his breath came out in harsh gasps.

"I need more," he said, his voice like gravel.

She nodded and allowed him to reach between them, to put his hand inside her panties and touch her.

"Oooh, God, Nick!" she cried out, her head thrown back as he played with her. She lifted her head when he withdrew his finger. Her heart nearly skipped a beat when she watched in fascination as he lifted his finger to his mouth and tasted it.

His face descended, his mouth lowering until it was so near hers she could smell the sweet smell of coconut and her own essence that lingered on his breath.

His lips touched hers, and his tongue delved into her mouth, transferring the taste to Sinclair. As though he had the right.

Her eyes drifted closed as his unique scent reached out and claimed her, even as his mouth did the same. Even as he had, long before this night.

She shoved the thought away, only wanting to concentrate on the here and now, and the way he was making her feel.

He smelled…tasted *so, so* good. A mixture of coconut and…man.

And me, she thought, a feminine smile stretching her lips.

The man part had her senses reeling and her vagina,

with a mind of its own…clenching, as though in anticipation of something more. She doubted that any woman *could* be anything but ready around Nick Kealoha.

He was lethal.

As he lay a light siege upon her mouth, his body hot, hard, pressing into hers, the scent surrounding her, she willingly gave in to his demands.

Hard, slamming…feral.

It was a wild, heady rush of need that slammed over her, had her moaning into their joined mouths, their bodies creating a dance of their own.

Before Sinclair realized what she was doing, the wild, unrepentant need that rolled over her had her rolling her pelvis forward and rocking back and forth in earnest against his thickness, a thickness that stole her breath.

The kiss took on an explosive quality.

Wild, hot, he devoured her mouth, tugging and dragging her lips within his, making love to her mouth in a way that made her lose her mind. Thoughts of how good he could make other parts of her feel rushed over her like a wild cascade of water.

He broke the kiss and she whimpered, trying to recapture his mouth, but he brought her close, his hand on her head, bringing it to his chest.

His heartbeat was thudding wildly against her face.

He was just as affected by their intimacy as she was.

Although he broke the kiss, he didn't ease her away. His body was still tightly crushed against hers, his shaft hard, pressed insistently against her stomach.

Their breaths were harsh. And both reflected a need neither was able to deny.

"Come home with me tonight."

The words were a rumble against her ear. A request this time.

Shocked, she couldn't move, much less form a coherent word.

She had only known the man for about a week, truly, despite the fact that they'd been in communication for going on seven months.

She chewed her bottom lip, remembering, thinking.

When he had showed her where his parents had met and had fallen in love, she'd seen the emotion in his eyes. She knew part of that emotion was from the loss of his mother. But she also knew there was a part of that emotion in his eyes that had to do with the way his parents had kept the fact that their biological father wasn't the man they'd called Dad for all of their lives.

The pain was raw and had made her reevaluate what she'd believed before, from their first contact and his reasons for doing so, to what had brought her out to the ranch to get rid of him, write a check and "Act like it never happened," as he'd said.

She felt…uncomfortable. A part of her, ashamed.

Nick had been an enigma to her, in the short time of their acquaintance. She'd briefly seen past the playboy he presented to the world to the cowboy who simply loved his land…

Yet, did she know him well enough to allow him to

do to her what his eyes…his kisses, promised would be unlike anything she'd ever experienced?

She wasn't here to get her groove back. She was here for her Wildes.

"This has nothing to do with them. This is you and me."

His voice had a hard edge that jerked Sinclair out of her thoughts.

She glanced up at him, licking her lips. She swallowed deeply.

He grasped her by the chin, forcing her to lift her head, forcing her to look deeply into his enigmatic blue eyes.

"And it comes down to the simple fact that you want me, Sinclair. You want me…almost as much as I want you."

He bent his head and recaptured her lips with his, briefly making a shudder rack her body.

When he released her, she was limp.

"As much as I've wanted you from the moment we began to communicate… It's fated… We are fated. Just give in to what we both have been waiting for…needing."

She glanced down at his open hand as he waited for her to place her palm within his.

Could this be happening?

Could she allow something like this to happen? With a man she barely knew…

She placed her hand within his much larger one.

His large, callused, work-worn hand grasped hers, holding it tightly. Even that sent shivers through her.

She imagined how those work-roughened hands would feel against her naked body.

Oh, God… She barely suppressed a shiver.

He didn't wait for her response.

He already knew. He'd known, just as she had, from the first moment they'd met.

Chapter 17

"You're one of the most sensual women I've ever met, ever known…"

She felt his hand on her shoulder as he came up behind her, his fingers toying with the thin T-strap of her dress. All of the air from the room seemed to be sucked out of it and Sinclair was left gasping, desperate for air.

"Shh, it's okay, baby. I'll take care of you. You trust me, don't you?"

He breathed the words against her neck, his honey-sweetened breath blowing warm against her ear. She inhaled sharply. When he kept still, unmoving, she slowly bobbed her head up and down.

"Completely untapped sensuality." His hypnotic, seductive voice was mesmerizing as he continued both his verbal and sensual assault.

She dragged in a fortifying breath of air and held it as his big fingers moved from the strap to ease around the front and cup one of her breasts within his large, able hand.

An air of expectancy had surrounded them as they'd driven back from the Rusty Nail, the out-of-the-way restaurant he'd taken her to. One that neither one of them attempted to "talk" their way around.

Both had known exactly what was going to happen, and the level of intensity, from the second they'd met until now…before they'd even met, had led them to this moment.

The time they had been communicating, before her arrival had been a buildup, a slow, wickedly hot foreplay of sorts that now had Sinclair so ready for him, she knew if they didn't make love… The thought of what would happen if they didn't escaped her mind when she felt his tongue work small circles around the lobe of her ear before laving a hot trail around and down the back of her neck.

"Mmm," she moaned against the wicked sensation.

"Do you like that? The way my tongue feels against your skin?"

Her voice in her throat, she was unable to answer, could only nod her head in agreement.

When they'd entered the grounds of the ranch, he'd driven directly to the house, yet he hadn't pulled his vehicle up to the main entry, surprising Sinclair.

The ranch house was a veritable mansion. And although she'd expected there would be more than the traditional two entry points into the home, she'd had no idea that Nick had his own entrance

He'd caught her surprise, and explained that there were what he called "master entries." Besides the front and rear entries, there were three others...one for each "master" suite: his father's, brother and sister-in-law's and his.

"For privacy," he'd said, briefly turning his attention to her as he parked the truck and shut the engine off.

In the dark cab, his blue eyes seemed to sear a hole directly into her, straight to her soul.

Coming around to her side, he held out a hand for her to take and again she placed hers within his and allowed him to lead her away.

He'd only turned on one small outside light, which gave just enough illumination to allow her to see enough so that she didn't stumble over her own feet.

Not that she would, with the hold he kept on her hand.

Sinclair felt strangely...safe, with him.

As they entered his massive suite, she squinted, trying to get a visual of what was a home within a home. His suite appeared larger than her condo back in Wyoming.

Yet when she tried, he purposely moved her away, blocking the full view of the room. He turned her toward the floor-to-ceiling windows that overlooked a picturesque view of the land and held her, mesmerized, in front of him.

Sinclair felt his hand move to her waist and stop in front of her mons, the silk of her dress doing nothing as protection against the heat of his palm.

"Raw, untapped sexual vitality," he rasped, both his words and tone putting her into a sensual coma.

Her body felt fluid and rigid at the same time.

A strange yet heady dichotomy of feeling.

He pulled her closer to his body, allowing her to feel the hot, hard, length of his erection against her buttocks.

Electric heat swamped her entire body, bringing a deep and staining blush she felt head to toe....

She needed this. As much as a part of her knew she was blurring the lines of professionalism and personal. Hell, she'd blown that line up. This was way beyond that.

This man had somehow imbedded himself into her very psyche.

"You want this as much as I do, Sinclair. Give in to me. Like you never have...for another man..." His deep voice breathed the words against her neck.

"Tell me you want it. That you want what you know I can give you," he boldly declared.

She licked excruciatingly dry lips, unable to say a word. Unable to admit that she wanted everything she knew he could give her, everything she'd dreamed about. And more.

She felt herself leaning back against him, as though some magnetic field was surrounding him...her, forcing her close, so close she—

She knew she should walk away, stop this before it could go any further, yet knew that would be an exercise in futility.

To make love with him would be an erotic exorcism....

She inhaled a hitched breath when he glided his hand

under her dress. His big hand on her bare thigh tickled the sensitive skin and stopped a hairbreadth from the band of her panties at the top of her thigh.

His fingers toyed around the thin ribbon, rubbing lightly back and forth until she felt her moisture increase, her panties now uncomfortably moist.

Her head was spinning and her body was already on fire.

And he'd barely touched her.

When he began to tug her panties down, she nearly sagged against him.

God, this is wrong....so wrong, so wrong, so... The cascading thought trickled in her mind.

Only to immediately have another override it.

But it feels...so good, so good, so...

When he fingered aside the edge of her panties and one thick finger brushed over the lower segment of her vagina, brushing over the hair, she nearly came.

From just that touch.

She felt her panties being pulled down, past her bottom, low enough so that he had better...access to that part of her that needed, desperately needed, to feel his torrid touch.

Sinclair held her breath, waiting to feel his finger. What he'd done in the car had been just a hint of what he—

Her mental imaging came to a halt. "Oooooh," she moaned at the feel of his finger inside her clenching heat.

Her eyes closed and her head sank back against the rock-hard chest that was now her pillow.

"I need to…play with you. Will you let me do that to you, with you, baby?"

She swallowed deeply. Dear God, what did he mean?

His hands were still, and cautiously she bobbed her head up and down in assent.

She heard his grunt of satisfaction.

Obviously that was what he needed before he would go on.

Seconds later she felt the hot stroke of his fingertips as he began to…play. Brushing back and forth against her mons, skimming over her clit that she felt engorging, as he began to *play* with her.

She moaned, her eyes fluttering closed as she bit down hard on her lower lip, nearly drawing blood as her heartbeat pounded and her vagina throbbed.

The moment Nick's fingers touched the core of her femininity he felt her clench and her body buck against his.

He knew she was questioning the sanity of what he was doing to her. Knew it as though he were inside her mind, reading it.

Just as he knew she wanted him as badly as he wanted her.

So responsive. She was so damn responsive.

Playing with her was going to be an experience unlike any other….

"Easy, baby…we've just begun." He whispered the words from clenched teeth.

His job to seduce her was becoming more and more

difficult. He silently counted to ten as he continued to play, needing to keep his libido from going into over-drive. Although he knew it was too late for that; his cock was as hard as granite as it pressed against her back.

They were both still fully clothed, and had only ex-changed kisses…hot kisses, to be sure. Scalding-hot, make-his-dick-rock-hard kisses. But kisses nonetheless.

And with any other woman he could kiss and caress until he had driven her wild with need, so that when it came time to press and stroke, it would take only a few hard driving pounds and he'd take his lover over the edge.

Yet he knew it would take all of his considerable willpower to keep from coming himself before he got in her good.

Damn.

When he felt the sweet trickle of her cream against his fingers, he groaned against her neck. He brought her body closer to his, forced her nearer…his one hand lightly circling her throat.

Not enough to hurt her.

Just enough to claim her.

She mewled low in her throat, a kittenish sound as her head lolled back against his chest. His fingers continued to toy and play with her, while he yanked her panties down far enough past her plump buttocks to give him ac-cess to her, but not far enough that she could move away.

Captive.

He needed this to last. He felt his shaft throb.

He grit his teeth and with iron control forced his cock into submission.

"Do you like what I'm doing to you, Sin?" he grunted, barely able to speak. Without giving her a chance to respond beyond a shaky nod of her head, he pressed his finger deep inside her clenching heat.

One lone…long finger. One teasing, tormenting finger was all it took.

Deeper he delved, his finger easing inside her vagina, slowly, yet piercing it roughly. She bucked as heat surged through her body.

"God, you're so damn tight."

He added a second finger, easing it into her sex, and she cried out, her insides clenching and releasing against the hot, dual invasion, her entire body on fire.

Warmth gushed out, partly easing his thrusting fingers as they slid deeper, teasing the inner walls, until he was knuckles-deep inside her.

"Oooh, Nick…" The words were little more than a gush of sound as she felt even more of her own wetness ease from her body.

She felt more than heard his groan against her neck. She was on fire for him. In the position she was in, turned away from him, she was glad for the privacy. The thought of making eye contact with him was one she couldn't fathom. She knew in her eyes he would see her desperate need for him.

"I need more, Sinclair." His voice was rough. "So much more. I'm sorry…I can't wait," he said and before she knew it, he'd flipped her around, catching her off guard.

She would have fallen onto the thick Persian rug had he not lifted her in his arms.

With sure strides he strode with her across the vast room, and moments later she found herself bouncing on the bed.

The room was impossibly dark, yet Sinclair could make out the shadowy figure of his big body as he turned away from the bed and bent to open a drawer nearby.

She heard the sound of his zipper…releasing. The sound of ripping foil…unsheathing.

"This won't be…easy," he promised, his voice so low and rough she moaned just from the gravelly sound. The more turned on he was, the more scratchy and rough his voice became. She never knew the sound of a man's voice in need could do what his did to her.

It was nearly unbearable; her need for him was high.

"But I promise you won't be disappointed."

When he lowered his body above hers, she felt more than saw him ease her panties down the rest of the way, lifting her as he removed them completely from her body.

She was on fire for him, yet surprised at the way he'd carefully removed her panties. She'd feared he'd rip them from her.

He laughed roughly and her eyes sought his in the dark.

"They're too pretty to rip," he whispered hotly into her ear.

The teasing way he said it, coupled with the fact that he'd read her mind, strangely brought a hot blush to her cheeks.

She laughed with him, softly, intimately, in the dark.

"Thanks…they're my favorite," she admitted softly.

"Oh yeah?" he asked. "I like them, too. Peach looks pretty against your golden skin," he said huskily.

Although the words were negligible, and shouldn't have turned her on, they did.

God, everything the man said…everything he did, turned her on.

"Thank you," she said and felt the blush creep again along her skin. The soft pillow talk was the kind that was strangely intimate.

Something lovers said to one another that shouldn't be hot, but damn if it wasn't.

She inhaled a deep breath as he nosed his face against the side of her neck. She turned her head against the soft, silk-covered pillow. His unique scent was on the pillow, as well.

She felt her essence as it eased down her center.

The scent of him was surrounding her, containing her within a sensual box.

She lay back further on the bed as he followed her down, his body blanketing hers.

When he hitched her leg up to wrap around his waist, she inhaled a startled breath.

When she felt the press of his shaft at her entry she exhaled the pent-up breath in one long *whoosh* of air.

She swallowed. When he'd held her close she'd felt

the length of his erection, but now, unrestrained and sheathed, she knew it to be thicker and longer than she'd thought.

One part of her was afraid to feel it…to touch it and gauge the true length and girth, knowing he was well endowed and worried about him fitting inside her. The other part of her was eager to feel his weight in her hand. She decided that she'd wait to feel it inside her.

"But first, let me make sure you're ready for me," he said, his voice low, so low it was a deep gravelly sound, sensually abrasive against her nerve endings.

When she felt the press of one lone, thick finger slowly invading her heat, she inhaled yet another deep steadying breath. He added a second finger. Slowly he pressed inside her, until he was to the second knuckle.

"Oooh," she whimpered, her voice barely a whisper, and he paused.

He lowered his head and pressed his mouth close to her ear. "Baby…are you okay? God, you're so tight even on my finger," he said, the intimate words brushing against her skin.

She swallowed and nodded her head. Although he'd pressed inside her moments before, this time he'd added a second finger. "It's…been a while. That's all," she said, feeling her cheeks heat at the words.

"I'll be gentle with you. I want this to be good for you," he said.

His words, plus the feel of his thick finger swirling around her clitoris, not only helped to calm her, but brought forth a renewed moisture from her body as it prepared itself for him.

She'd been intimate with men before. But she'd broken up with her last boyfriend soon after law school after realizing he'd only been with her because of her connection with the wealthy Wildes. After that stinging realization she'd thrown herself fully into work.

Love…sex, had been the furthest thing from her mind.

Until she'd met Nick.

Chapter 18

He leaned over to capture her mouth with his.

The kiss he gave her was long, hot and sensual.

Whimpering, Sinclair's tongue came out to meet his. Dueling, lapping and suckling each other, it was one of the most erotic kisses she'd ever had.

He reached a hand up and placed it around the base of her neck, tugging her mouth closer to his. He slanted his head for a better angle, his tongue growing more insistent…aggressive…as it laid siege to her mouth.

"Oh, God, your lips taste so good…so sweet," he growled when he finally broke the connection with her mouth.

With one final twirl of his talented fingers against her blood-thickening bud, he slowly withdrew from her clenching sheath.

"How are you doing, baby?" he asked.

The question seemed even more intimate voiced in the dark room with nothing but the overhead moon shining through the skylight above to cast shaded illumination.

"I'm…I'm okay," she said, finally able to speak.

"Good, then you'll feel even better, soon…."

Before she'd had time to catch the meaning of his sexy promise, he'd eased his big body down onto hers, lifted her legs up and away from where he'd wrapped them around his waist, draped them over his shoulders and moved his head between her parted thighs.

"Nick…?" she questioned, her heart thumping harshly out of control in her chest. Was he going to…?

Her back arched sharply off the soft comforter and a cry tumbled from her lips with the first stroke of his tongue against her folds.

She felt his fingers as they separated her lips, felt the heat of his breath as he blew it, softly, against her heated center.

"Ohhhh…" She let out a soft, low moan when finally she felt his tongue, thick, rough, as he lapped once from the end of her cleft to the tip of her clit.

She held her breath, keeping it held, as she waited.

Her wait wasn't long. He dragged her pulsing bud into his mouth and lightly toyed with it.

"Nick…" His name was a husky moan of pure bliss.

He suckled her, delivering low licks and hot sensual glides of his tongue against her until she felt every nerve ending on fire. Her head tossed back and forth, her body grinding against his face.

"You like that, huh, baby?" He growled the question/statement against her mound, his voice so low and throaty she could barely make out the words.

"Hmm, *yesssssss,*" she breathed. Her body was on fire. She squirmed around his talented tongue, whimpering when her soft cries elicited a deep male chuckle, one that rumbled and vibrated against her lips as he continued his sensual assault.

On and on he…played with her. He used tongue, lips and thick fingers to toy with her, making the most intimate type of love until Sinclair felt her orgasm hovering, threatening to break.

She pried her eyes open and looked down at him. His dark head between her thighs was such an intimate visual she closed her eyes again, her body slumping back against the thick comforter.

His mouth fastened one last time on her clit, his tongue giving one final stroke, and she went over the edge.

Her body lifted and she reached down, grasped the sides of his face and lightly ground into him, unable to do anything else, the moment overtaking her as she gloried in the feel of his tongue.

As she ground against him, her soft hands on either side of his face, Nick felt his own orgasm hovering.

Damn!

He'd always enjoyed pleasuring a woman in this way,

but as much as he had enjoyed it in the past, it was nothing compared to what he felt now.

She was so responsive, so damn responsive.

He'd only meant to prepare her for his invasion. After pressing a finger inside her warmth he'd soon realized that although she was not a virgin, her experience had been limited.

His cock had gone hard to granite-hard in 2.2 seconds.

And when he'd felt her dew cover his fingers, he'd had to taste it. The smell, taste and feel of her all added up to turning his world upside down.

It was then he knew that he had to take her over the edge. He wanted to see her when she orgasmed, wanted to experience it with her. He knew that once he was inside her, taking his pleasure from her beautiful, sexy little body, he wouldn't be able to think beyond the feel of her.

He watched through half-closed lids as her orgasm swept over her.

She was a beautiful woman. God, she was so beautiful.

He felt something beyond his cock react. A sharp pang hit him so hard in the chest he nearly moved off her and clutched his heart.

God…what was she doing to him?

When she finally lay limp, her head on the pillow, her eyes closed, he reached down and made sure the condom was still on his cock.

Rising, he covered her, lifting her legs and wrapping them around his waist.

"I think you're ready for me now, baby," he whispered, the words barely recognizable even to his own ears.

A soft smile spread her pretty little bow-shaped lips apart. "Yeah…"

He would have laughed a masculine laugh of satisfaction at the look on her face, knowing he was the one to put it there. His cock, if possible, hardened even more.

"I'll try to go easy on you," he said huskily.

Her eyes snapped opened when he began to press inside her.

He knew, without ego, he was large. And she was so damn small.

He'd have to ease inside her, take his time—

The thought cut off the moment she clamped down on his shaft, her walls milking him the minute he entered.

He bit off a curse and grasped both of her wrists within his hand, lifting them and bringing them above her body

The action brought her small breasts together and his hot gaze centered on them.

"Ohhhh." The distressful little cries were wrought from her lips, yet he pressed on.

"Just hold on, baby, it'll be okay," he promised roughly.

Unable to resist the temptation of her pretty brown breasts with their tight, perky, dark wine cherry-topped nipples, he bent and brought one into his mouth and sucked.

Hard.

At the same time he pressed all the way home, deep inside her tight and clenching walls, until he felt his balls tap against the soft underside of her butt.

"Nick!"

He took one of her breasts within his mouth, and with his free hand, palmed the other. Perfect.

She was perfect in every way.

Her breast, although small, was big enough to spill over his hand cupped beneath it. He tugged on her nipple, groaning when she began to grind against him in sexual excitement.

As he suckled one breast, the hand that held its twin pinched and massaged the other, before alternating, his mouth giving up the connection with one only to transfer its attention to the other.

"Nick. Nick. Nick… Nick…" she cried in little whimpers as he made love to her curvy body.

Her tight little squirms, mewls of sexual distress and overall feel of her body against his was one he feared would make him end their lovemaking *way* before he wanted to.

"Baby, please… Stop. Moving. Just for a minute." He grunted the words, the admission torn from him as he dragged his mouth from her sweet breasts.

He was afraid if she continued to move the way she was, it would be over in a stroke or two.

She felt incredible. Perfect for him.

It had been very taut pressing in, and she fit him tighter than any woman ever had. It was unlike anything he'd ever felt before.

For the first time in his adult life, he resented the use of the condom he'd automatically donned. Although he knew it was a necessary evil, he wanted to feel her naked on his shaft.

He doubted he would have lasted longer than a few strokes if they hadn't used one.

If anything, that imagery immediately made him even harder. He shoved the notion away.

No time for any thoughts beyond the way he felt, balls deep, inside her sweet warm center.

"So damn good… Feel so good, baby." He knew his words were barely intelligible, but at the moment he was damn near beyond human speech.

He bent and captured her lips with his. He kissed her slowly, passionately, the connection he felt with her unlike any he'd ever felt with another.

He released her hands and allowed her to let them drop to the bed.

One arm reached behind him to stroke against the soft skin of her thigh where her legs were wrapped around his waist. Although she felt good like that, her legs wrapped around his waist, he wanted to go even deeper inside her. He needed a different angle to penetrate her in the way he wanted…the way he needed.

It was almost a desperate need to reach as far into her as he could. Until they melded so tightly it was impossible to tell where one left off and the other began.

He wanted to *breathe* inside her.

If possible, his cock grew longer, harder, at the thought.

He deftly untangled her legs from their position, and in one smooth move, pushed them up and to the side, so that her beautiful body was spread out in front of him, her legs to either side of his as he began to stroke inside her sweetness.

"You feel so good, so good. This is the real deal," he grunted. His breathing grew ragged as he held her legs apart to receive him as he plunged deep inside her body.

He took her with a gentleness he was far from feeling, trying his best to hold back, fearing if he took her the way he wanted, he'd hurt her.

"Nick... God... Nick...please," she panted, her voice a coarse whisper as she pleaded for something he instinctively knew she was too inexperienced to know what it was.

She needed him to go harder.

He smiled into her throat, nipping the tender flesh there out of instinct, clamping down with a small sting, he knew, but not so much to hurt her.

Just to claim what was his.

As he picked up the tempo and his strokes became harder, stronger, he growled against the hollow of her throat. Her wet, velvet walls opened and closed in a sweet welcoming rhythm as he pumped inside her relentlessly, testing her to see how much she could take, still holding back.

He felt the sweat began to drip from his body, dropping down upon hers.

He didn't know how long he could hold back. As much as he was giving her…he needed to give her more. Needed to take more.

He grit his teeth as he continued to stroke, grunts of pleasure escaping his mouth as he drove into her sweet welcoming heat.

His body began to shake with the need to go deeper. Harder…

He felt her soft hands on the sides of his face and opened his eyes, staring down at her beautiful face.

He groaned at what he saw. Her limpid brown eyes stared at him, passion-filled and begging for…more.

"I…I need you, Nick," she whispered and her soft little cries were nearly his undoing.

Still, as he stroked inside her, he kept his thrust measured, tempered.

He didn't unleash all of his passion on her.

"And I'm giving you all of me, baby," he said, laughing roughly, hearing the need in his own voice, one that reflected what he saw in her eyes, felt in the quivering of her body against his, the warmth of her flesh burning into his.

When she lifted her body from the bed and pressed into him, grinding herself against him, she pulled his head down to meet hers. Moments before their lips connected she whispered hoarsely, "I need you deeper, baby."

With a harsh groan he latched on to her lips at the same time his hands grasped her curvy hips.

He feathered his tongue back and forth over hers, licking across the seam, asking for entry. With a moan she granted it, and swiftly he buried his tongue within. As he invaded her mouth and as she opened her mouth to his, her legs widened even more to accept more of him. To accommodate him.

He ran his tongue within the moist walls of her mouth, the length behind her perfect teeth before plunging his tongue deeply back within her

Against her mouth he replied, "Hold on, it won't be… easy."

"Hmm," she moaned, her lips curving upward even as he took them with his own.

When he'd first pressed inside her, Sinclair felt as though he was tearing into her, his shaft so thick, hard and long she'd felt it in her womb.

Now her eyes drifted closed and a soft breath of need escaped her lips as he kissed her, made love to her mouth and began to increase his depth of stroke.

It had taken a few minutes for her to adjust to him, but he turned her on so much, her own cream helped ease the way for him to feed her more of himself.

It wasn't long before she was greedy to feel all of him. She could tell he was holding back, afraid he'd hurt her.

Maybe she should be afraid, as well; his cock was so hard and thick, she felt stuffed.

When he pulled her tighter, kissing her, one of his

hands reached down, curved to the swell of her hip and palmed one of her buttocks, bringing her closer as he ground and stroked inside her.

"Hmm, yessss," she moaned helplessly.

"Like that?" he asked, the intimate question making the moment even more erotic as he stroked and rolled inside her. She could only nod her head up and down, the feeling too intense to allow her to say much more than a moan.

Her arms crept up and circled his neck, pulling him down closer as he continued to pin her to the bed, as he stroked inside her, his thrust becoming longer, more... intense.

Her breath caught in her throat when he angled her body to his, agilely moving her, shifting her slightly even as he continued stroking. Although the feeling was incredible, it was as though he were searching for something.

"Ahhhh!" she cried harshly into the dark room when he found what he was looking for. "Oh, my God...oh, my God...oh, my God..." The litany continued as he stroked inside her heat. "Oh, please, keep it right there... Nick, pleeeeease," she keened long and harsh as the side of his shaft brushed against a softness inside her body.

When she arched her body up in surprise, she heard his masculine rumble of satisfaction. He knew *exactly* what he'd done.

No man had ever found her...spot.

She swallowed deeply, her body no longer hers. It

now solely belonged to the man who was making it feel so incredibly good.

Again, she heard his low masculine laughter.

It brought out an answering, very feminine need to respond in kind.

She'd only read about it, but...

She reached down, blindly, and with only a few awkward moves, finally was able to grasp what she wanted.

She held his balls lightly in her hand and feathered caresses over them.

"This will be over before we both want it, if you keep that up." He growled the words, his voice nearly inhuman it was so low, like sandpaper, it was so gravelly.

"Turnabout and all that," she laughed softly, barely able to keep it together. What they were doing to each other was something she couldn't have imagined in her most erotic dreams.

He removed her hand and replaced it with his.

Nick moved his hand around and inserted it between them, finding her clit and rubbing it softly as he rocked her, on and on, until she felt her orgasm hovering.

When he found her clitoris, her soft laugh turned to a moaning scream. He slammed his mouth against hers, grinding against her, and within seconds she released.

Her cries of completion echoed his as he followed her into ecstasy's path, the tsunami they'd created together, sweeping them both along in its wake.

Chapter 19

"The Aloha Keiki, your family's foundation... How did that start?"

She felt his body tense and immediately regretted asking.

Sinclair knew through her research that not only was the Kealoha ranch the most profitable family-owned-and-operated ranch on the islands, but that the foundation his family ran in his mother's honor was one of the most successful nonprofit organizations that helped youth on the island.

He'd shown her the fields and orchards, and during her time on the ranch she'd also met some of the adults and young people who volunteered. But she hadn't heard from him the way it had started.

She had a desire to know as much as she could about

him, knowing their time was short together— She shooed that thought aside.

"I…I'm sorry. If you don't want to talk about it, I understand."

She felt his body relax, and his hand continue the stroking of her skin, in the way that he'd been doing since they'd come down from the erotic wave their mutual orgasm had taken them to.

It had been a long time before either one of them could speak, and when they'd finally been able to, it had been the talk of new lovers.

Pillow talk. Talk about nothing of any real importance; just enjoying the feel of sated bodies against each other and soft voices spoken in hushed tones.

Whereas before, in her limited experience, Sinclair had always felt a bit uneasy in the moments after sex. Not sure what to say… She'd never known the "protocol."

Neither of the two men she'd been with had made her feel in the least the way Nick had. To even compare them was a joke.

He was definitely in a league of his own.

Before, what had constituted pillow talk with her two previous lovers, had ended up an aborted attempt at best.

But it wasn't just her. It had been them, as well. They hadn't been much more…experienced in post-coital chatter than she had been.

So, she thought she should feel more…intimidated with Nick.

He was so much more experienced than her.

Additionally, he'd definitely been with more partners than she had. There was no way a man as fine as he was hadn't had plenty of women throwing themselves at him.

Not to mention his sexual skill… What he'd done to her body, how he'd made her feel…

"It started before my mother passed away, as you know. We've kept it going, built it and nourished it to see it thrive in the way it is now."

She forced herself to put her thoughts to the back of her mind so that she could focus on him speaking.

She listened as he, haltingly at first, started to talk about the foundation.

When she mentioned the foundation, a part of Nick had rebelled. He hadn't wanted reality to come barging in on the pleasure they'd just given one another. He hadn't wanted to think of anyone or anything else beyond the incredible, erotic encounter that had just occurred between them.

It was no secret that he was the one considered of the two brothers to be the "clam."

He'd never been what you would call "comfortable" opening up and baring his soul.

Just wasn't his thing.

With the exception of with his brother, it was not going to happen. And even with Key, the closest person to him, there were times when he felt more at ease keeping a barrier erected, or at least trying to.

Not that his brother had ever allowed that, he thought,

a small smile lifting his mouth. And to that end, most people thought he played it loose and easy.

He'd always been comfortable with folks thinking he either was a player or had no emotional depth. He'd never really given a damn what others had thought of him.

He frowned, recalling the words of one of his partners.

"Nick, you are unable to connect emotionally." She'd hurled the words and they'd bounced off him like eggs on a non-stick fry pan.

No effect.

It wasn't as though he didn't care about other's feelings; he didn't like hurting people, and particularly not women. The truth was that he had a very soft spot for the gentler sex. He simply preferred remaining...unattached.

He didn't need a psychotherapy session to tell him why that was. He knew it was because of his parents, what he'd always known to be true about them: that although they loved each other, there'd been something... missing.

He shoved the thoughts aside.

He glanced down at the top of Sinclair's head, her soft curls now lying in thick waves on her shoulders. With her, he found himself strangely okay with talking about his family, at least in this limited way.

Nick laughed, remembering his brother's reaction when the reality show's film crew had come to the ranch.

"What?" Her soft question brought him out of his thoughts.

"My brother wasn't exactly...welcoming when they

first came. The film crew, that is. But Dad and I knew it was a necessary evil. Eventually, Key saw it the same way. The end justified the means."

"'Necessary evil'?" she questioned, tilting her head to the side.

"Not exactly my feelings. Didn't really want them around, truth be told, but the idea didn't piss me off like it did my brother. You would have thought the hounds of hell had been loosed on the property with the way Key acted." He laughed outright. "Yeah, but then he remembered why he'd allowed the TV film crew on the ranch in the first place."

"And why was that?"

He smiled, thinking of his mother…his father and brother. Their history and love for Hawaii.

He recited the words that were ingrained in his mind, heart and soul.

"Family, ranch and the preservation of Hawaii," he murmured.

Although it was dark, he could feel her confusion.

"Those were the reasons Key finally agreed to allow the film crew on the ranch. Kinda became the family battle cry," he said, and she laughed softly along with his low chuckle.

"I remember reading something online that stated the reasons for the show were to make more money for the ranch…and maybe exploit two of Hawaii's 'dynamic duo,'" she murmured when their chuckles had died out.

Nick heard the question behind the teasing words.

He groaned. "Please, if you like the fact that my

brother likes you…don't mention that ridiculous nickname," he advised. "That is a surefire way of getting
you escorted off the premises," he finished.

"I'll keep that in mind," she laughed. "At any rate,
you're the one with the more…" Her voice trailed off and
instead of being offended he laughed outright.

"I'm the 'player'? Yeah, I know," he replied.

He was well aware of his reputation as a "player."
Hell, his own brother at times bought into the image
he so carefully portrayed. Although he knew that his
twin knew him well, and was also aware that behind
the player image was a man who loved his family, his
ranch and Hawaii as much as he did, and took it just as
seriously.

And in reality, he'd carefully built up the playboy
image as a way to discourage anyone from trying to
get too close to him. Although his mother and father
loved each other, had always showed love to him and
his brother, a part of Nick had seen something else in his
mother's eyes when she'd thought no one was looking.

"Yeah, a lot of folks think that. I don't really give a
damn, though. By any means necessary." He paused,
considering, before he continued to speak.

"The attention from the show brought in an awareness
we couldn't have paid for—an awareness to the Aloha
Keiki foundation our mother started. We wanted to
honor her and to see her dream, her desire, to help those
who are less fortunate prosper. And if my 'player' image
helped bring in donations, who am I to complain?"

"Of course. All those beautiful women hanging

around the ranch, fawning over your every word, was a sacrifice you were willing to make, huh?"

She surprised yet another laugh from him. "Exactly!"

Her tinkling responding laughter made his smile linger.

He felt an odd little feeling in the pit of his stomach.

He'd been getting more of them lately, funny little feelings in his stomach; his chest would even ache oddly at times. There were even times he felt his heartbeat literally race, times when he wasn't doing anything extraneous.

He frowned. He'd visited the family doc a month ago and knew he was healthy as a "damn horse," as Dr. Pedersen had put it. Heartbeat regular. Blood pressure normal. Cholesterol count perfect.

When he felt her snuggle deeper into him, as she burrowed against his side, he felt the smile return to his face, and the odd thought that he was ill passed.

It was such a sexy thing to do, he thought, snuggling into him in the way she had.

"And we have my sister-in-law to thank for the extra publicity for the foundation," he said, bringing her closer to his body. If that were even possible.

"How so?"

"She made sure that when it came to the PR for the show, it was included that the true reasons we agreed to another season was for the foundation. Initially we kept that within the family—our real reasons. The executive producers thought it made for good PR when Sonia 'accidentally' let it slip 'our real reasons.'"

"Accidentally on purpose?" she said and he grinned.

"Yeah, something like that. We trusted her. And with that, she helped the foundation prosper even more," he said, pride in his voice for both the foundation and the woman he now called sister.

"It's an amazing foundation," she murmured, her words creating a warm spot in his heart. He felt his... feelings...for her grow.

"Thank you. Its purpose is to help disadvantaged youth by bringing in donations to the poorer communities on the island."

"It's admirable. Not just that your mother started it, but that her family loved her and their community so much they sacrificed to see it prosper," she stated simply, the sincerity in her words real, touching.

Nick felt that weird ache in his chest again.

Unconsciously he clutched at his chest.

She reached up, as though she, too, had felt the pang... or felt his pain, and placed her hand over his. Their intertwined hands lay on his chest.

He frowned down at her. The only other person he'd ever experienced that type of mental kinship with had been his brother.

The fact that she knew the information showed that beyond finding out what she needed to to help her Wildes, there had been more to her research than a way to "take care of" the Kealoha problem.

"Yeah," he began, and she burrowed even closer, bringing an unknown smile to his face.

"The money we get comes from both donations as well as what we generate from the farms," he told her.

"Farms? Like the one you showed me, the orchard?" she asked, softly interrupting him.

He nodded.

"Yes, like the one I showed you, baby. We have a few other ones. New ones we are creating on other islands to benefit other communities. All the proceeds are designated, targeted and used to help with agriculture for the youth, for them to learn a usable skill. It's also used for scholarship opportunities for the high school students who want to attend a college or university," he continued. "But the kids know to tap into the resources they have to help out."

"Through their volunteerism," she said, and he nodded. She'd been paying attention.

"Sure do." He was aware of the pride in his voice. "Most do so in the gardens, but we have a small group who come to the ranch and one of the hands supervises them, gives them tasks to do, to help them learn more about ranching."

"You're an amazing man, Nickolas Kealoha," she murmured, her voice thick with sleep.

Her words caused another kick to his heart.

He didn't want to think of her in those terms. Soon, she would be leaving the ranch. Soon, she would be leaving him.

The thought brought back that pang in his heart, this one so strong he grumbled. She sleepily laid a hand over his chest.

In the center of his heart.
He bit back a curse.
He was falling in love with her.

Chapter 20

"What a nice way to enjoy an afternoon break," she breathed, the words fluttering against his chest as soon as her heart had calmed and she could speak again.

She felt more than heard his rumble of laughter.

She groaned. "That sounded so flippant, didn't it?" she said as she lifted away from him to gaze down at his face.

The smile on his handsome face made her catch her breath.

He was such a beautiful man, and when he smiled, his entire face lit up, making him breathtaking.

He was the perfect specimen of manhood.

"Hey, I like it," he said and reached up to touch one of the curls that had, as usual, managed to ignore her attempts to keep it restrained.

His vigorous lovemaking had made sure the rest of her hair had followed suit, and now it hung around her shoulders in kinky, curly waves on her shoulders.

It was the weekend, and although a rancher's workday didn't preclude the weekend, she was surprised when he'd asked her if she'd be interested in going out with him. She'd agreed and they'd spent the day together.

He'd taken her to one of the floral orchards, as well as one of the small gardens that provided his mother's foundation with its supply. She'd been touched when he had brought her to the foundation gardens, knowing how much it meant to him, to his family. A part of her heart opened up that much more to him, despite her desire to take it one day at a time and enjoy what they had without bringing too much...*feeling* into it.

She feared it was too late for that.

"Oh, Lord, I must look a mess!" she said with a groan, brushing aside the gloomier thoughts and searching, in vain, for a ponytail holder.

"I like how you smile, laugh...how comfortable you are with me. I also like this," he said, continuing to finger the curl. "Why don't you leave your hair down more?"

She smiled over her shoulder at him as she pulled her shirt over her head and continued her search. "Not exactly the image I try to project, at least back home," she said, distracted.

"And what is that? What kind of image is it you're trying to maintain?"

He got up and tugged his jeans up the length of his

legs. She stopped as the sight of him dressing was nearly as exciting as him undressing. He caught her staring and gave her a knowing look, which made her blush.

"I happen to like the way you look, too," he said, reading her thoughts. They held glances, mutual smiles on their faces. He leaned over and kissed her softly before patting her naked rear end.

"Finish getting dressed, woman. We have the entire day ahead of us," he said and her smile returned.

Later.

Later they could talk about what was going on between them. How he made her feel.

She felt the changes within herself, knew that no matter what the outcome of her visit here, on a personal level, she wasn't the same woman.

"The image I 'try to project'?" she mimicked, not really paying attention to what she was saying in her vain attempt at finding the band to secure her hair.

She pulled her panties up her legs as she considered the question.

"I don't know. Just one of a professional woman, I guess, is as good as any way of describing it."

"I would think that would go with the territory, what with your profession. Don't your Wilde Boys treat you that way? Like a professional woman? Or do they still see you as the little girl who grew up on the ranch?" he asked.

She turned to look at him, wondering if there was anything in his question besides a simple question.

His look was the same. From his expression it didn't

look as though he was mocking her, or the men. She re-laxed yet felt tense, not because of anything on his part, but her own.

Her Wilde Boys.

She hadn't thought of them in that way in a while. She bit on her bottom lip, uncomfortable with the thought.

He caught the way she was worrying her lip and his head tilted to the side.

"You okay, babe?"

"Um. Yeah. Just thinking, that's all," she said as she finished buckling her pink wedge-heeled sandal. "They do. It's not that the brothers don't treat me as a profes-sional. They do. It's just hard sometimes, growing up in the same hometown, with the same people," she finished.

It wasn't always easy to voice her feelings to her-self, as she'd been struggling with the conflicting feel-ings she'd been having lately regarding her career, the Wilde Ranch and the feeling that she was ready, in a lot of ways, to leave.

She'd felt a sense of guilt when she realized that for as much as she loved the Wildes, her life on the ranch and in her hometown, since the death of her father she'd found herself ready to move on.

"You know, sometimes change is good. Doesn't have to be bad, or make you feel guilt-ridden, either. We all need change sometimes," he said.

Again it was as though he was reading her mind.

Her gaze flew his way with a deep frown on her face. God, had she been that transparent? Had her feelings been that clear to read?

And if he'd guessed, did that mean the Wildes had known, as well? Had that been the reason Nate had encouraged her to fly to Hawaii, and not only that, encouraged her to take a small vacation?

Nick wasn't even looking at her, she noticed, her body relaxing at the realization. He was busy buttoning the remaining buttons on his shirt.

She exhaled. Despite the sexy sight of his muscled chest exposed to her, the beautiful lightly tanned skin thick and corded with muscle, she closed her eyes.

She thought back over her last conversation with Nate.

"So do you think this is the best course of action?" she asked as she leaned against the kitchen counter, her arms braced on the granite countertop as she held the mug of coffee between her hands.

The kitchen was the gathering place for the Wildes.

All three of the brothers lived on the ranch, and over the past year they'd completed the construction on the west wing, so that the house—mansion, really—had an extra three thousand square feet added to it overall, as each master suite for the couples had been expanded.

The brothers' rooms had already been large by most home standards, but now each one was like a home within a home, each room reminding Sinclair of a luxurious suite in an upscale hotel, complete with its own small kitchen area.

It was a retreat, and although they rarely did so, if at any time the brothers and their wives chose to break away from the family for a night or weekend on their own, their private suites allowed them the luxury without feeling stifled or restricted due to size.

There was no expense the brothers had spared. No expense when it came to their new wives and their new lives together. As much as she loved them, there had been a small part of Sinclair that envied them their love.

"I think if *you* feel it is, that's good enough for me, Sinclair. You know that I—we, the entire Wilde clan, trusts your judgment," Nate replied.

He brought his own coffee mug in hand over to where she sat perched on one of the stools near the low, circular granite counter they often ate and drank around, in an informal setting.

He eased his long frame onto one of the tall bar-stool-style chairs.

"So... Nate, what you're saying is, it's up to me, this decision?" she asked and bit down on the bottom of her lip.

Nate laughed. "Okay, so what's up?" he asked before taking a drink of his coffee and grimacing. "Told Holt to stay the hell away from the coffeemaker," he complained.

She smiled, despite her ambivalent feelings, before her face became serious again.

"How do you know there *is* anything wrong?" she asked, putting her own cup to her mouth. She grimaced, as well. Holt really did make the worst coffee she'd ever had.

"Little sis, whenever you bite your lip, I know something is on your mind," he said with a smile.

For whatever reason, that brought tears to her eyes, tears she fought against.

"Hey, what's wrong? Something is really troubling you!" he said.

Sinclair could only shake her head.

Smiling a shaky smile, she began to speak. "It's this whole situation," she told him.

He frowned. "With the Kealohas? You don't need to be upset about that. We have confidence in you, and at the end of the day, we've had to deal with situations a lot more complicated than this. We'll survive."

"It's not that so much as…one Kealoha, to be exact," she finally admitted.

And with that, she opened up to Nate in ways she hadn't even admitted to herself. Telling him that she was confident in her abilities, that it was Nick she was having problems with. Not the Kealohas as a family.

Just one Kealoha.

Nate listened carefully, without interrupting her once.

She poured it all out. The situation with the Kealohas was one she could handle, she assured Nate. In fact she had no issues with anyone in the family. After her initial interaction with Keanu Kealoha, it had been Nick Kealoha with whom she had dealt. And *that* was the problem. How Nick…affected her.

When she finally finished, she felt as though a weight had been lifted from her shoulders.

With an odd look on his face, one she didn't understand completely, he gathered her to his big chest and hugged her. When he set her apart from him and stared so intently into her eyes, she felt the rash of tears return.

"What?"

"Nothing. It's just wonderful seeing how you've grown into this amazingly wonderful young woman, so confident, so smart and capable..." He stopped, laughing and shaking his head. "And so beautiful, that if I hadn't grown up with you like a sister, and didn't have a wonderful woman I love more than life itself, I'd be a little jealous of Nick Kealoha," he said to her utter astonishment.

"What are you talking about, Nate Wilde?"

He smiled. The smile had been tilted down at the corner, as though he was sad in some way.

She frowned. If she didn't know better, she could have sworn in Nate's eyes was a mist....

"Nate?" Her voice cracked on his name.

"We have all the confidence in the world in you. Go to Hawaii. Do the Wildes proud as we know you will, baby girl," he said and hugged her.

They small-talked after that, and when he left her to go to work, she stared after him, a bemused look on her face, wondering what he knew that she didn't.

It was as though he was saying goodbye...with his blessing.

Unaware, a tear slipped down her face as she watched him walk away.

Now, as she watched Nick Kealoha get dressed, waiting for her to finish, a part of her wondered what Nate had known that she hadn't.

"Ready, babe?" he asked, smiling and holding out a hand for her to take. She again brushed aside the odd feelings she got whenever she thought too hard about the Wildes.

With a nod she placed her hand in his and allowed him to lead the way.

Chapter 21

"Ever saved a horse and ridden a cowboy instead?"

"Nick! You scared the hell—" The rest of her rant was smothered in his kiss. With a blissful sigh, she turned, wrapped her arms around his neck and kissed him back in earnest. Really getting into his kiss, she stood on tiptoe to get better access.

He didn't just kiss. He made love to her mouth, just like he made love to her. Hot, sweet and incredibly naughty.

She smiled around his kiss. He broke away, staring down at her.

"What?" he asked, his finger coming up to trace the smile.

She shook her head, "Nothing. Just thinking."

"About?" he asked, releasing her. She sighed, turning to face the documents on her desk.

Sinclair had been in the middle of going over the final documents she was sending off to the Wildes for their inspection before giving it to Nick for him and his family to go over.

His gaze went to the papers on the desk she used at the ranch.

It had been more than a week since they'd gone over it, and she had begun to wonder if Nick was holding something back. Every time she mentioned the settlement he would either divert her attention with lovemaking...or divert her attention with lovemaking.

She frowned. The man made her feel like the easiest woman on the planet, she thought.

He turned and caught the frown. Leaning down, he kissed it away.

"What's up? I know that look," he said, yet something in his eyes troubled her.

"You know what's up, Nick. What I can't figure out is why?"

"Why, what?" he asked, but she saw the way he evaded her eyes.

"That right *there!* Every time I bring up the settlement you go weird on me!"

When he folded his arms over his chest and stared at her, looking at her as though *she* was the one being strange, she'd had it.

She stomped her foot, feeling all of ten years old, but she was at her wit's end. Although Nate hadn't said anything, nor had any of the others, she knew they must be wondering why a matter that should have taken three days, a week tops, had turned into a weeks-long adventure.

The fact that no one had actually said anything to her was a mystery she didn't understand, but the fact remained: she needed to wrap it up.

Every day she was in Hawaii, the Kealohas were making it harder and harder for her to think of the time she'd have to leave.

"Come on, baby, we have to deal with this. I don't like that I have to keep trying to get you to look at something that will benefit you. The settlement is fair, but if there is something you don't like, you or the family, let me know, I'll let the Wildes know and—"

"What?" she asked, her frown returning.

"What if I told you I don't want a damn thing from your Wilde Boys? My family and I are fine."

She frowned and moved toward him. She placed a hand on his arm and looked up at him. "What's going on? What are you talking about? I'm well aware of your family's wealth, baby. No one is saying you 'need' anything from the Wildes," Sinclair said, shying away from calling them her Wilde Boys without even being aware that she did.

She hadn't referred to the brothers in that way for a while yet that she was aware of.

"Listen. We need to talk. Really talk," he said, taking her hand and guiding her toward the desk.

He opened his mouth and began to speak, his eyes locked on hers.

"I…well… See, the thing is," he began and stopped.

"Baby…are you okay?" she asked and he looked at her, helpless, looking lost.

"Nick?" she asked, her voice lowering, fear threading it.

"I…I want to make love to you, baby," he blurted the words. "I've needed you all day. You know how I get," he said and buried his head in her neck, his hands shaky as they rested on her waist.

Even as she allowed him to lift her enough to remove her panties, she felt the fine tremble in his hands.

"Nick, baby, we really need to go over the papers," she moaned as his finger delved inside her, withdrawing her cream, her body already preparing for his.

Before she could question him further, before she realized that he had once again diverted her attention, her panties were on the floor and he was reaching for the box of condoms they kept in her desk.

It hadn't been the first time he'd taken her in her makeshift office.

Condom donned, seconds later he was easing his thick, long length inside her welcoming body.

As he rolled his hips she accepted him, rocking into him, their bodies swiftly catching one another's rhythm. Natural-born lovers. She moaned as he groaned, their voices sighs of passion even in sync.

Lazily she rolled back and forth on his shaft, her body calling to his.

The lazy sway of their lovemaking didn't stop the inferno from building and it wasn't long before their orgasms hit simultaneously.

As he came, he wrapped his big arms around her waist, bringing her close as he pumped, once, twice, three more times, his voice muffled as he growled his release.

It was long moments before her heartbeat returned to normal.

Not just because of the mind-blowing orgasm, but also because of what she thought she'd heard him growl against her neck as he came.

"God, I love you," he moaned in a heartfelt whisper against her neck.

Simple. Direct.

And, oh, God…she loved him, too.

Tears threatened to fall.

"How's everything going, Sinclair? Haven't heard from you. Thought I'd give you a ring, girlfriend!"

Sinclair smiled, leaned back against the soft down cushions on the bed in her hotel room and withdrew her glasses from her nose.

"Hey, Yaz girl, how are you?" she said, glad for the interruption, her mind not on the brief she was finishing, but on Nick, the Kealohas, the Wildes…and the tangled mess she found herself in.

"I'm doing well, babies are doing well, too," she said and Sinclair smiled.

Yasmine was pregnant, and had recently learned that it wasn't one Wilde, but two little Wildes growing in her tummy, a fact that had Holt, her husband, with his chest swollen with pride.

"How's Holt?" she asked, ready to giggle. Holt and Yasmine had always cracked her up, as Holt had a wild sense of humor and could make anyone laugh with a few well-chosen words.

"Girl, he got his chest all poked out, proud, like he *did* something!" she said.

"Yeah, well, girl, he kinda did help. I mean, it takes two and all that."

"Yes. True. And that is exactly what I'm talking about. It takes *two*. Not one. *Two,*" she emphasized. "With the way my husband is walking around the ranch talking about how potent he is…how, if it wasn't for his Superman sperm— What, baby? I'm on the phone, I *can't* talk to you!" she said, yelling at Holt, one hand covering the mouthpiece. Despite the ambivalent feelings Sinclair had due to her own personal situation, she fought back a laugh.

Holt and Yasmine always, without fail, cracked her up. When Yasmine got back on the phone, the two women caught up on what had been going on at the ranch in her absence.

Finally she opened up with Yasmine. She hadn't told anyone what had been happening between her and Nick, not because she didn't feel like she could, but mainly because she hadn't figured out her own feelings. Until he'd told her he loved her.

She knew without doubt she'd heard it.

After she spilled her guts, told Yasmine everything, she waited. Then said, "I love him, Yaz. I really love him."

She waited for the scream.

It wasn't a long wait.

"*Oh. My. God!* They were right, Althea and Nate were right! Wahooo! Wait until I tell them. Oh. My. *God!*"

Despite the yelling and hollering, Sinclair picked up on something, a frown making her sit straighter.

"Nate and Althea were right? What do you mean, Althea and Nate were right?" she asked.

She wondered if Yaz's pregnancy was affecting her in some weird way she had never heard of. There was a pause, and she could feel Yasmine's discomfort.

"Oh, shoot. Me and my big mouth," she mumbled.

Oh, no. This wasn't good.

Of all the women, Yasmine was not only the worst to know a secret, she was the worst to keep a secret. Which was why she knew that what she was about to hear wasn't going to be something she necessarily wanted to hear.

"You might as well come clean, Yasmine. Cat's darn well out of the bag. Almost, anyway. Besides…you know you always feel better when you do," Sinclair said, cajoling the woman and not feeling the least bit bad when Yasmine, in her pregnancy-induced emotional state started to whine, sniffing while saying, in a very small voice that Holt was going to get her when he found out. Then she stopped to giggle at her own words, repeating them.

"Holt's gonna *get* me," she said around her giggles. "Maybe the babies will come quicker if he does!" she said, her mind already on something else.

"Focus, Yasmine," Sinclair said, trying not to snap at the pregnant woman, knowing that it was truly the hormones racing in her body that made her the way she was. Kind of…

"Okay," said Yasmine, sobering. She began to whine again, begging Sinclair not tell, and on and on…until Sinclair forced the truth out of the woman. Finally.

And the truth made her face blanch.

When Sinclair was able to get off the phone, adroitly avoiding an agreement not to tell the brothers, she in fact wondered who she should confront first. The three men whom she considered brothers…

Or the one she was beginning to love like one. The one who was the identical twin brother of the man she was in love with.

All four men were not only in cahoots with each other, regarding the Wildes and the property, the inheritance and all, but were also responsible for her being there in the first place. They were responsible for all of the time she had been there, and for purposely throwing her and Nick together.

Chapter 22

"I messed up, Key."

The admission was made reluctantly as Nick found his brother in one of the stables, after looking for him the entire day.

He'd wrestled with the issue of the Wildes and, more importantly, Sinclair, for the better part of the day.

Hell, he'd been wrestling with it for longer, much longer than that.

"I was wondering when you would come and find me," his brother replied mildly.

"Am I missing something here?"

"No, Pica. I just figured you would make your way here eventually. Grab a broom. Menial work clears your head," he said.

With a frown Nick grabbed a broom as his brother'd asked, and began to help him clean out a stall.

"Okay, so what gives? Why are you doing 'menial' work, as you put it? Everything okay with you and Sonia?" Nick asked, putting his own troubles to the side to make sure his family was okay.

Key threw him a smile. It was strained in the corners and Nick began to worry. "We're fine, Pika... No fears. Just shoot. What's on your mind?"

Again, Nick hesitated. Two times his brother had called him by his nickname, one was to purely tick him off, the other time was as if something was on his mind, bothering him.

He continued to sweep after Key refused to say anything more.

Nick spilled his guts.

Opened up to his brother in ways he never had with anyone else.

He told him how he felt about their parents, how he felt about Clint Wilde.

"I know you don't feel the same way that I do, Key. I get that. And, man, damn if I know why it affected me like that—that he never found out about us—but it did," he finished, glancing toward his brother.

"Did?"

Nick laughed. "Yeah, did. Crazy thing is, it doesn't even matter anymore," he said, running a hand over the back of his head. "And the reason for that is because of Sinclair," he admitted, his voice gruff, raw.

His brother said nothing, just continued to work, but

Nick knew he was paying close attention to what he was saying.

"I love her more than I thought I could ever love a woman. More than I thought it was possible to love," he said, and turned away. As much as he loved his brother, he felt exposed admitting his feelings about Sinclair in such an open way.

"Have you told her?" Key asked.

Nick shook his head no even before he'd fully asked the question.

"No. Don't know how. Hell of it is, I don't know if she feels the same way."

"Man, come on. You know the woman loves you. Hell, the whole damn ranch knows how you two feel about each other. Damn sure you haven't hidden it."

"I tried. Damn if I didn't. It's just that whenever we're together, it's like there's no one else. I love her more than I love the A'kela Ranch."

When he made that admission the brothers locked gazes. The emotion in his eyes was one he couldn't hide, not from his twin. The A'kela was not simply their ranch, it was them, who they were.

By saying he loved her more than the A'kela it was clear that his words were deep and heartfelt.

Key smiled. The smile was one of relief, mixed with something more.

He grabbed his brother and hugged him. They hugged for long moments before Nick lightly shoved him, making him laugh as he pushed his twin away.

"I can't keep her here forever. She has to know the truth soon."

"Don't be an idiot like I was with Sonia. Tell her. Don't let her leave without telling her. And tell her the truth—that you don't want the Wildes' ranch. That the Kealohas don't want the Wyoming Wilde Ranch."

Nick blew out a breath after patting his brother on the back. "Wish it was that simple. How the hell do you tell somebody you love that you've been keeping something from them, just because you wanted to get to know them...? That what you felt from the first time you spoke was something you'd never felt for another person before?"

"Just like that, brother," Key said.

The brothers locked gazes. Nick laughed. "Just like that, huh?"

"But before you do, there's something I've got to tell you. And I don't think you're going to like it," he warned, rubbing his hand over the back of his neck.

Although he felt dread, Nick recognized the gesture, one that he himself made whenever he was unsure of himself.

"Oh, hell...what is it? Don't tell me... You and the Wildes have been talking?"

The look Key gave him was almost worth the ass-whooping Nick was going to give his brother for going behind his back to talk to the three men Nick had professed to dislike.

Even as he began to roll up his sleeves, Nick knew

that as far as ass-whoopings went, this one would be fair and evenly matched.

"Aw, hell. Okay, let's get this over with so I can tell you everything and you can get your woman," Key grumbled and began to roll up his own sleeves.

No one knew him like his brother. It was a natural thing to do, to go to him. Even if his brother was an ass sometimes.

Chapter 23

She was on fire with need for him, unsure if she could hold off until they got back to either her hotel or his home.

Her glance fell over him. In the dim light of his truck cab, she was still able to make out how able his big hands looked as they gripped the wheel.

He must have felt her gaze as he turned enough to glance over at her. He smiled and reached over to lift her hand up and bring it to his mouth.

He surprised her when he turned it over and placed a kiss in the center of her palm.

She felt the…intimacy of the kiss. Erotic. Different. But so hot.

"Today was amazing. Don't know the last time I enjoyed myself like that, Sin."

She smiled at his words. When he'd first called her the nickname it had startled her, so different than what she'd been used to in the way of nicknames.

"Sin," he'd called her.

She was the sensible one. The responsible one. Definitely not a woman with a nickname like Sin.

No. She was the girl who studied, sailed through undergrad and law school easily. The one who worked hard and…worked hard.

Family had come first. Her own. She and her father, as it had been the two of them since her mother's passing years ago. Then her extended family. The Wildes.

Now that her father had passed away, what kept her at the Wilde Ranch was the Wildes themselves. After everything they'd done for her, from the financial assistance that had allowed her to go to law school, to the position as their attorney, she felt a sense of…obligation to them.

Sensible Sinclair. That was who she was and, more importantly, who she was comfortable being.

She turned away from Nick, but allowed him to keep her hand within his much bigger one.

Sin.

One side of her lips hitched upward into a secret little smile. Lord knew the man had made her sin more than a little bit. And she'd loved every minute of it, she thought, holding back a sigh.

She'd decided to talk to Key first, after hearing everything that Yasmine told her that happened, from the beginning.

Assuming her friend's pregnancy-addled brain had it right, a part of her felt gratitude for what they'd done.

But she still was unsure about how Nick was going to respond. She knew that his dislike for the Wildes ran deep… How was she going to tell him that his brother had been in communication with them from the get-go?

Yasmine had informed her that after his initial communication, Nate had reached out and, believing he was speaking to Nick—and not realizing it was Keanu he was talking to—had told him that they—the Wildes—looked forward to meeting the Kealohas, and had nothing to hide. They wanted the brothers to come to the Wilde Ranch to see it. He'd invited them to become part of the family, to move to the ranch if they had a desire to.

The Wyoming Wilde Ranch would welcome the twins with open arms, sharing in the wealth as they knew their father would want them to.

She'd wondered how and what they'd had to do with her, and how the second part of their odd but well-meaning plot had evolved.

She bit her lip, wondering how she was going to tell Nick that part, as well. It got kind of tricky, there.

She'd searched for him all day and finally found him in town, and the two had decided to come back to the A'kela. It was then she noticed that he was quiet.

More quiet than usual.

"Baby…can we talk?" she asked, and he turned to her, his blue eyes filled with lust and need. A heady combination; one she knew too well.

"Yeah…after."

She knew what "after" meant, and felt her body respond. She also knew something was on his mind, as well.

"I promise, baby. We'll talk…after," he said, his eyes holding hers, and she nodded. Again he brought her hand to his lips to place a soft kiss in the palm.

For some reason the sweet gesture brought tears to her eyes. She batted them away, and stared out the window, wondering how he was going to feel when she told him.

The truck came to a smooth halt and Sinclair began to unbuckle her seat belt when his hand on hers made her stop. She turned to face him, a question on her lips.

The look in his eyes made her ask, "Baby…what's wrong?" Dread pooled in her gut, afraid she knew the answer.

"I think you're right. You've been right all along," he said, searching her eyes. "Let's talk." He squared his shoulders. "Hell, let's get it over with now. I don't want to wait," he finished.

"Here?" she asked, wondering at the urgency. It was as though he thought he was going to face the firing squad.

She swallowed. Afraid. She knew that what she had to tell him he wasn't going to want to hear. He may even question her motives, but she had to tell him.

She was opening her mouth to tell him when he forestalled her.

"My brother…the Wildes…have all been in communication with each other, for the entire time we have been," he began.

Promptly her mouth formed a perfect *O*.... He knew.

She listened as he told her, his head hung low as though he was afraid, or ashamed. She felt the love she had for him grow even more, and the decision she had made, to stay at the ranch, she prayed was one he wanted, as well.

"Baby, it's okay. I know everything!" she said, but realized he wasn't listening. When he continued speaking, she frowned. The happiness she felt began to fade as disbelief took its place as he continued to speak.

Nick knew that if he didn't say it in one big rush, get it all out, he would never do it.

After he and his brother had nearly come to blows, he knew it was the least he could do to tell her the truth, the entire truth.

As his brother had told him, he knew he could hold back, not tell her of his part in it, how he'd already decided long before she came that he wanted nothing from the Wildes. But if he did, there would be no other reason for their continued communication.

"And I couldn't do that. So I went along with it, pretended I still wanted to sue the Wildes," he said, finishing stoically. He hadn't been able to look at her, not since he'd seen the crestfallen look cross her pretty face.

"Why did you do that? Why did you lie like that?" she asked, her voice so low he felt, for the first time in his adult life, like damn near bawling, she was pulling at his emotions so.

"I'm sorry. It was the only way..." He stopped.

"Revenge was that important to you? To waste my time...?"

"No. It was because I was already in love with you. Which is what my brother saw. Which is why he went along with the Wildes in sending you out here, as well," he said, praying to God it was as his brother had said: that the Wildes had seen her love for him, as well, the spark they hoped would flourish for a woman they considered a sister.

She frowned. "Okay, let me get this straight. Your brother and the Wildes put this all together because your brother believed you were in love with me, and the Wildes thought I was in love with you?"

He nodded his head.

She chewed her bottom lip, frowning at him.

"And did you? I mean, uh, were you falling in love with me then?"

Her eyes were lowered and he was unable to see the look in them. But he heard the uncertainty, the small catch.

"God, yes, baby. I didn't know it, but I knew I'd never felt like that in my life. It wasn't long before I started to suspect I was in love with you."

"Falling-down-drunk kinda love?" she asked.

He felt a grin tug at the corner of his mouth. Humor was good. If she was laughing...

"Falling-down, begging-please-baby-please in love with you," he said, hope blossoming.

"Well...I guess since you put it that way," she said and

laughed when he dragged her across the seat and into his lap, swallowing her laughter with a kiss.

"Oooh, yessss." The wail of pleasure was ripped from her lips in one long hiss.

For long, hot moments, there was nothing to be heard in the stable but the sound of horses softly neighing, providing background noise to what was going on in one of the empty stalls.

"Shush, baby. You're going to wake up the ranch if you keep that up," Nick said, his deep voice husky and low, intimate as it and he brushed over her skin. "But I do like how you respond," he said.

Before she knew what he was going to do, she felt him stroke deep inside her in one fatal hot slide, deep inside her welcoming warmth.

They hadn't made it to the ranch before he was dragging her inside the stable, a wicked grin on his face.

"We haven't done it here, yet. Want to?" he'd asked, a wicked smile on his handsome face.

The request was just what she'd needed. Light, sexy and fun…before she would have to tell him something he wouldn't want to hear.

Now, as he stroked inside her, she met him thrust for thrust, as they made love facing each other, his legs thrown over hers as she rode him.

"You're my perfect match, baby…you know that?" he asked, his voice low and rumbly, just the way she liked it when he was really turned on.

She grinned, asking, "Oh yeah…how's that? Because

I can do this?" she asked, performing a move that had him growling so low she giggled. Her giggle turned into a long purr of satisfaction when he mimicked the move. With a twist.

He lifted her, easily, and stroked inside her, and soon there was no time for laughter. There was nothing but pleasure and moans, sighs of delight and hot glides of skin against skin.

He placed his hands on either side of her face, his face strained with pleasure. She gasped as he stroked, widening her legs to take as much of him as she could, his shaft thick, long and hard as it speared inside her wet, welcoming warmth.

When she tried to look away, the feelings, both physical and emotional, became overwhelming, too much for her to handle, too intense, but he wouldn't allow her that luxury.

"Yesss. Oh, God, yes," she moaned, her head rolling back in pleasure.

"You like that, baby? Like the way I make you feel?" He breathed the words more than said them and she bobbed her head up and down in eager agreement.

"Yes, Nick, I do…I love it, and I love you," she cried out sharply when he pinched her nipple before grasping the turgid tip into his mouth and sucking away the small pain.

"Good…so good," she moaned. Her body was on fire with need, and he was the one, the only one, who could put out the flames.

When he widened her legs, she took in a breath. The

tip of his shaft was tapping against her bottom as he deep-stroked her. "Before I give you what you need…" he said, and pushed a fraction deeper inside her. "You have to tell me what I want to hear," he said, taking her nipple back into his mouth, swirling his tongue around it.

Her mouth went dry. "Wh…what are you talking about?" Coherent speech was nearly behind her.

"The Wildes. Tell me I'm more important to you than they are. Tell me they are no longer your Wilde Boys," he said.

She inhaled a shuddering breath. Not because of his demand, but because he pressed inside her quivering lips.

She was shaking so badly, so filled with lust and need…and love for this man, that she would say anything, do anything, for him.

"Tell me I'm the only man you'll ever need, ever want." His voice was like graveled sand. Low. Demanding…yet filled with uncertainty.

"God, yes, yes, yes!" she cried in agreement, hearing his chuckle as he lifted her hips and began to press all the way inside. "Baby, I love you," she cried, and forced the red haze of lust to the side so she could see her man.

She grasped the sides of his face this time, forcing him to look into her eyes.

"I love you. Only you."

His eyes closed briefly. When they opened again, the blaze of love in their deep blue depths was nearly blinding in its intensity.

"That's what I wanted to hear, baby," he said, no triumph in his voice. Only love.

At the moment of climax she felt it, reached for it, her eyes glued to his, swaying as they reached the summit together.

On a long wailing cry she released as he did, with him inside her...

"I love you, baby. God, I love you!" he shouted and she allowed the tears of emotion associated with good loving and even more than that, being in love, to freely fall.

* * * * *

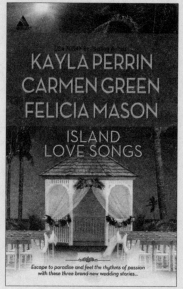

REQUEST YOUR FREE BOOKS!

2 FREE NOVELS
PLUS 2 *FREE GIFTS!*

KIMANI™
ROMANCE

Love's ultimate destination!

YES! Please send me 2 FREE Harlequin® Kimani™ Romance novels and my 2 FREE gifts (gifts are worth about $10). After receiving them, if I don't wish to receive any more books, I can return the shipping statement marked "cancel." If I don't cancel, I will receive 4 brand-new novels every month and be billed just $5.19 per book in the U.S. or $5.74 per book in Canada. That's a savings of at least 20% off the cover price. It's quite a bargain! Shipping and handling is just 50¢ per book in the U.S. and 75¢ per book in Canada.* I understand that accepting the 2 free books and gifts places me under no obligation to buy anything. I can always return a shipment and cancel at any time. Even if I never buy another book, the two free books and gifts are mine to keep forever.

168/368 XDN F4XC

Name	(PLEASE PRINT)	
Address		Apt. #
City	State/Prov.	Zip/Postal Code

Signature (if under 18, a parent or guardian must sign)

Mail to the **Harlequin® Reader Service:**
IN U.S.A.: P.O. Box 1867, Buffalo, NY 14240-1867
IN CANADA: P.O. Box 609, Fort Erie, Ontario L2A 5X3

Want to try two free books from another line?
Call 1-800-873-8635 or visit www.ReaderService.com.

* Terms and prices subject to change without notice. Prices do not include applicable taxes. Sales tax applicable in N.Y. Canadian residents will be charged applicable taxes. Offer not valid in Quebec. This offer is limited to one order per household. Not valid for current subscribers to Harlequin® Kimani™ Romance books. All orders subject to credit approval. Credit or debit balances in a customer's account(s) may be offset by any other outstanding balance owed by or to the customer. Please allow 4 to 6 weeks for delivery. Offer available while quantities last.

Your Privacy—The Harlequin® Reader Service is committed to protecting your privacy. Our Privacy Policy is available online at www.ReaderService.com or upon request from the Harlequin Reader Service.

We make a portion of our mailing list available to reputable third parties that offer products we believe may interest you. If you prefer that we not exchange your name with third parties, or if you wish to clarify or modify your communication preferences, please visit us at www.ReaderService.com/consumerchoice or write to us at Harlequin Reader Service Preference Service, P.O. Box 9062, Buffalo, NY 14269. Include your complete name and address.

KROM13R